BLACK
EDEN

Dr. Mildred Dumàs

Library of Congress Control Number: 2019931440
ISBN-13:   Paperback: 978-1-64398-647-0

Printed in the United States of America

LitFire
PUBLISHING

LitFire LLC
1-800-511-9787
www.litfirepublishing.com
order@litfirepublishing.com

ACKNOWLEDGEMENTS

First, I would like to thank God for giving me a creative mind to entertain, inform, enlighten, and educate others with my various writings.

For legal advice, I would like to thank Richard Lloyd, retired Assistant U. S. Attorney for the Southern District of Illinois.

Thanks also to Tonie Griffith, retired Administrative Law Judge for putting me in touch with Mick Ballard, Broker of the Inland Empire, who told me how to have my characters legally steal property.

I would like to, also, thank my sister, Annie Dumas-McGraw, Retired Courtroom Deputy Clerk for the Southern District of Illinois, for assisting me with other legal matters, and for standing by when my computer kept breaking down during the writing of this novel. And thanks to my good friend, spiritual advisor, and the lady who directs all of my plays, Chaplain-In-Training, Naomi Stenson, for standing by just in case Annie's computer decided to break down, also.

My sincere thanks to retired English teacher, Robert Jones, for proofing Black Eden. I hope you have successfully recuperated from the ordeal.

To my good friend, Linda Cayce-Chamberlin, thanks so much for explaining the process of *Searching for a Pastor, and to* Elder Michael Shumpert *for explaining the basics for receiving a new member into the church.*

I would also like to thank my advisor at LitFire Publishing, Ryan Fox, and other LitFire personnel for so patiently guiding me through the process of getting this novel ready for publication.

I am so grateful to all of you. God Bless.

DEDICATIONS

I would like to dedicate this book to my late parents: Mr. and Mrs. Joe Ben and Mary Dumas; my extremely talented daughter, D'Ambara Merriweather, also deceased; and other family members who have supported me in all of my endeavors throughout the years—especially my two sisters, Ethel and Annie, who come to the premier productions of my plays.

I would also like to dedicate this book to Miss Rochelle Williams who has been producing my plays and hosting book signings for my novels for many years—and to Dr. Elizabeth Marshall who provides the space.

This book is also dedicated to the many actresses and actors who have bravely stepped onto stages at theaters around the country to portray the characters in my plays.

May God bless and keep all of you.

Other Works by
Dr. Mildred Dumàs

<u>Novels</u>

BITTER INHERITANCE
FACADES
CHRISTMAS BLESSINGS

<u>Most Popular Plays</u>
(Entire list is too numerous to name)

THE POWER OF MY WILL
(Drama)

UNCLE RUFUS I AND II
(Mystery Comedies)

LOOKING FOR A MAN
(With Sylvia Roberts)
(Dramatic Comedy)

MY BROTHERS' BLOOD
(With Ernestine Harbour)
(Drama)

WHEN THE PAST COMES BACK…
(Drama)

THE GRIEVING WIDOWS' AUXILIARY I AND II
(Comedies)

A GATHERING OF FIRST LADIES
(Historical Drama)

Chapter One

"That church is the devil's playground."

He could hear his deceased wife's voice so clearly in his head, but this was his dream; this had been his dream for so many years he could not remember. She was gone now, so she had nothing to say about how he lived his life anymore.

God rest her soul.

He had to push on. It was just him and their son, Forrest, now, and he had to do what was right for him, and he knew deep down in his heart that he was doing the right thing.

Perspiration popped out all over his face. His once jet black, now almost completely gray, curly hair was drenched. The water ran from his brow, down over his high cheekbones—his paternal grandmother's contribution to his rugged, handsome features; she had been a full-blooded Choctaw Indian—then down his chest, under his armpits and onto his new blue, silk suit.

He felt as if he were drowning, being swallowed up by his own sweat. He felt faint, but he could not do that. That would certainly cinch it: his failure, his inadequacy, his inability to pastor a church like this—his dream of so many years.

He had to push through his discomfort.

The preacher wiped furiously at his drenched face with his freshly washed, starched and ironed handkerchief. He had washed and ironed it himself. He had to do that now since his wife had died. He had no one else to do it for him now, and she had impressed upon him the fact that any preacher worth his salt would not enter a pulpit without such an item on himself.

Handkerchiefs were not defunct as some people would like them to be, she reminded him. She also told him not to pay any attention to the ushers prancing around passing out those little, thin, paper tissues that would not hold up under a good preacher's sweat.

"Mine eyes have seen the coming of the Lord. In that great-getting up morning when the trumpet sounds, we're going to rise. Yes, we are, saints! We're going to rise up and walk. In that great getting-up morning when the dead in Christ shall rise, when the Lord comes down from glory to take His children home. Oh, what a day that will be. What a time! What a time we're going to have communing with our Lord! I want to be in that number. Do you want to be in that number, my brothers and sisters? Do you want to be in that number when He comes back to take His children home? Do you want to be among the blessed?"

"Yes, I do!" came a reply from one of the sisters in the audience.

"Communing with the Lord!" came another reply.

"Oh, yes! Yes, Lord!" came another.

Praise Him!" came another reply.

"Glory!" chimed in another.

"Hallelujah!" yelled another.

Most of the replies to the minister's rousing sermon came from the pews to the right of the dais—from the "Mothers' Bench," as it was appropriately called. Occupying the first two rows of pews to the right of the dais in First St. Marks Missionary Baptist Church were the elderly sisters, the diehards as they were known around First St. Marks.

Some of these ladies had been at the church since the doors first opened some sixty years earlier, and, as they had been heard to say: "We're going stay right here. We're planted right here at First St. Marks, no matter what, no matter who comes up in here trying to chase us out with a whole lot of unnecessary changes and other nonsense. We're staying right here, and we're going to fight for what we believe in, and that's that!"

And they had stood their ground. They had given some of the prior ministers of the church who had come in there trying to change some of the rules they had made for their organization—changes that made no sense whatsoever—*holy hell*. Some battles they had won; some they had not, but they had reached an agreeable compromise, and the elderly sisters of First St. Marks were satisfied.

If this preacher got the nod, it would be another wait-and-see operation.

Maybe this one, if he got the nod, would realize it would be to his advantage to work with First St. Marks' Mothers' Board.

That would make things easier for everybody, especially him.

The preacher was winding down his sermon, so his voice was at its peak, pounding home the Sunday morning message. It was a hard job. He had discovered that fact a few minutes after he took his text. He had to keep reminding himself that he was preaching his initiation sermon. That this was, indeed, Sunday morning service at the church he would give almost anything to pastor.

He had dreamed about this moment for so long. For years he had dreamed and prayed that he would someday have a chance to pastor this church, and now his opportunity had arrived, and he could not thank the Lord enough for this opportunity.

His heart was burning with thanks, with praise for the answering of this prayer that had been on his lips for so many years.

The Lord had put him in place, and now it was up to him to seal his fate with this life-long dream that had finally come true.

His initiation sermon . . . how was he doing? Was he passing the test? The response from the Mothers' Bench provided some semblance of encouragement.

The preacher turned toward his possible salvation in obtaining his goal and belted out the rest of his sermon. "I want to be in that number! Oh, yes, I do, church! I want to hear the Master say, 'Well done, my good and faithful servant! Well done! Well done, Benjamin! You fought a good fight! Your race on earth has been successfully run! Well done!'"

"Well done!" came a reply from the audience.

"A good fight!" shouted one of the mothers.

"Oh, yes, a good fight!" came another.

Come on, Sisters. Help me out here, Ben thought. "Well done! Mine eyes have seen the glory of the coming of the Lord!" he bellowed, ending his sermon.

There were a few more "Amens" and "Hallelujahs" from the Mothers' Bench and from some of the other parishioners who had been waiting all week to be filled with the Holy Ghost while listening to the audition sermon of this preacher who was aspiring to become their pastor.

He was here, and he had just finished his sermon.

Some thought he had done a credible job; others . . . well, the jury was still out as far as some of the other hopeful expectants were concerned. They would have to sleep on it.

There were others who had been waiting to hear the aspiring preacher's sermon also—for other reasons, however. Could he measure up? Was he the kind of person who would listen to reason? If not, could he be molded into that kind of person?

Would he fit into the plan?

The chairman of the deacon board, Gaston Davis, some of the other deacons, and the chairman of the trustee board of First St. Marks were debating that last question right then. Was this the right man for the job? Would this man fit into their plan? Would he pass the test?

"He's an okay preacher, I guess," Deacon Davis whispered to the man beside him.

"I guess," said Deacon Henry Sparks.

The Reverend Benjamin Thomas closed his Bible, picked up his handkerchief from the pulpit, and wiped frenziedly at his face. He stepped back and lowered his tall, lean frame into the dark-red, leather, high-backed minister's chair that sat immediately in back of the pulpit.

His arthritis was acting up. He hoped no one had noticed the slight limp when he rose to go to the pulpit. They might think he was too old to serve as their new pastor. He was just sixty-seven years old. He had many more good years left in him.

He had to do something about his failing knees. More exercise maybe. He had slacked off with his exercise. He had to get back into the habit.

In spite of the air conditioning in the building, and the fact that he was done with his sermon, perspiration still streamed from his pores. His deeply set dark brown eyes—so dark they almost looked black—were filled with wonderment.

He hoped they had not heard the pounding of his heart. He could not remember when he had been so nervous when delivering a sermon. He was a seasoned minister. He could not understand what the problem was. Maybe he shouldn't be here after all. Maybe . . .

"*Stop it,*" he whispered to himself. He had asked the Lord for this, and his prayers had been answered, and at this moment, that's all that mattered.

"Ask and it shall be given." He had no right to question the Lord after He had given him a blessing. And that's exactly what this was: a blessing. He has asked, and he had received, and he was grateful. He had to remain thankful and grateful and continue to praise the Lord for this blessing of all blessings.

The negative thoughts had to stop.

"Be careful what you ask for; you just might get it," was another saying he remembered quite well. His father, who had also been a minister until his death ten years earlier, had warned him about that one many times. "Sometimes what you want is not what the Lord wants for you, and neither is it what you need, Son" he would say.

But no, this was not a mistake. It was a blessing, plain and simple. *And I am* going to *bask in it—if I get the job, of course,* he thought. No, not if, but when he got the job. He had to think positively.

Chapter Two

"That was a powerful sermon, Dad," Forrest said, as he patted his father's knee encouragingly.

Forrest was a younger replica of his father. He sat to Ben's left in a chair that was a few inches shorter than the one in which his father sat. A few other associate ministers sat about them on the dais.

Forrest and his father worked together. They were a team.

Forrest was his father's right-hand man. He had been assistant pastor to him at The Greater Rock Missionary Baptist Church, in an adjourning city, for the past ten years. He had been appointed to the post even before he finished the seminary. It was their intention, or his father's intention anyway, to continue that practice here—if they got the post, of course.

Forrest was not sure he really wanted this for them. He had a gnawing feeling in the pit of his stomach about this one, and his mother had been opposed to his father even applying for this post.

He just didn't know.

I have to get this, Ben thought. The Pulpit Search Committee had to know that out of all the other ministers who had applied for the position, he was the best candidate. He was the best, and he had to make them realize that. They would be getting two-for-one really. They wouldn't have to worry about an assistant for him. His assistant was already built into the package.

"Thanks, son. They're just too quiet," Ben whispered.

"Maybe they're laid back Christians here.

"Don't think so."

Come to Jesus, Come to Jesus,

Come to Jesus just now, Just now;

The choir sang softly—a little too softly. Benjamin and Forrest Thomas were used to the noisy, knock-down-drag-out kind of church service: the real, shouting, foot-stomping, getting down, Baptist music. But regardless of how they were singing the song, it was Forrest's cue. His father always preached the sermon, and Forrest's job was to open the doors of the church.

"What are we doing here anyway, Dad?" Forrest asked his father. "It's just a feeling, but I still have doubts about whether we should be here."

"Let's wait and see if we get the appointment before we start passing judgment, Son."

"I'm not sure I want it. This place scares me. My gut is telling me *no.*"

"Don't be too hasty with your decision, Son. It might be worth our while."

"Love of money is the root of all evil, Dad. Or have you forgotten that?"

"Don't knock it until you've tried it, son."

He will save you, He will save you.

He will save you just now, just now.

The choir continued with another verse of the song. The director was staring at them now, an annoyed look on her face.

That woman scares me, too, Forrest thought. He rose and went to the pulpit.

Ben had been wanting First St. Marks even before the Rev. Simms and the other pastor before him had come. He had been keeping up with the happenings at First St. Marks and had wanted to put in his bid each time there was a vacancy, but Joan, his deceased wife, had been so set against it.

"That church is corrupt, the devil's playground, and I don't want to go near it. Those people are possessed," she told him and refused to discuss the matter again.

She had been dead for little over two years now. Ben missed his wife, but he welcomed the opportunity to live his life the way he wanted without having to answer to anyone. And what he wanted more than anything in the world right now was First St. Marks.

Forgive me, Joan, but I must do what is best for me, he thought as he surveyed his splendid surroundings from the vantage point of the dais of the place of his dreams. Here he was. He was on the hot seat, so to speak, but he was here. Whether he stayed was left up to him, and he was prepared to do whatever it took to make that happen.

The Lord had done His part, and now Ben had to do his.

He had never wanted anything more in his life. *Lord, please let what I did this morning solidify this appointment for me and my son. I thank you, and I give you all the praise, all the glory, and all the honor. Amen,* he prayed silently to himself, as his son ended the call-to-discipleship portion of the service.

No one came forward to give themselves to the Lord.

Had he not been profound enough in his sermon to inspire at least one person to come to Jesus?

He hoped that was not a bad sign.

He rose and went to the pulpit to give his closing remarks and the benediction.

Chapter Three

Ben and Forrest always made it a practice to stand at the front of the church to shake hands with the parishioners as they filed out after service. They would carry on this tradition here at First St. Marks as they had at Greater Rock, if, or course, they were chosen as the new ministerial staff.

They and the associate ministers stood in place now—their practice run so to speak. Both their minds were whirling. What kind of reception would they get from the people here at First St. Marks?

What did they think of my sermon? Did I pass the test? Ben thought.

Then the people were upon them.

"Wonderful sermon, Reverend."

"I enjoyed the sermon."

"Welcome, Reverend."

"It was very nice. I hope they choose you."

"Marvelous. Your sermon was simply marvelous, Reverend. Welcome."

"You're truly a dynamic speaker, Reverend Thomas."

The compliments and well wishes went on for a good while.

Forrest was getting his share of handshakes, too, as was the associate ministers, but it looked like his father was quite popular with this congregation. He felt proud, although he could not seem to shake the odd feeling in his stomach.

He smiled. He would have to heed his father's advice and stop being so negative.

Some of the congregation passed them by without a word. Some gave Ben a curt nod of the head as they passed, and some just shook their hands and kept walking.

But the majority stopped to interact with them. Ben knew there were going to be a few stragglers in the group, so he was prepared for their rebuffs. But if he had the nod from the majority, he felt safe.

But the people did not have the last say, did they? He had to wait for the nod from the Pastor's Search Committee.

But if the majority of the congregation liked his sermon, that should account for something.

Lord, please let this be a good sign, he thought.

"We'll call you," Deacon Davis, the man who had the last word in the matter, said as he and his wife—who smiled and gave them a curt nod--strolled past them.

Ben looked after the departing couple. The man had not even shaken his hand, just walked right past him with his curt remark. And was that all he had to say? "We'll call you." Ben wanted to know something now. At least get some indication that he might . . .

Take it easy, Ben, he thought. He had to remember that he was not calling the shots here. Not yet anyway. He had to wait for the Search Committee members to make up their minds—especially Deacon Gaston Davis.

It was a big church, over two thousand members, with so much to offer—including the biggest salary he had ever commanded in all his thirty-nine years of preaching. It would be a challenge, but one that he would welcome. One he would cherish. One he would covet...?

"You got it."

Ben and Forrest looked at the old woman who stood before them. A pair of piercing, fiery, wise, light blue eyes darted from one to the other of them, finally coming to rest on Benjamin.

She wore a simple black dress, a single strand of pearls, and small pearl earrings. She was tall and slightly built. Her hair was completely gray. She wore it in a bun in back of her head. A small black hat with a slight veil was perched atop her head. She was light-complexioned, her thin face lined with wrinkles. Her nose was long and pointed. She had thin lips and a protruding chin.

A White woman?

Of course, the church was so big, there had to be a few white parishioners. More and more churches were integrated nowadays, but he had heard that most, about ninety-five percent, were African American—most of them the higher echelon of the African American community.

No, he could tell now that he had gotten a closer look. She wasn't white, just another victim of circumstance.

"The appointment is yours. I saw it in my dreams last night. Welcome to First St. Marks. But don't accept the house. Tell them you want the parsonage next to the the church. It's safer," the woman continued.

Ben opened his mouth to respond, but the woman darted through the crowd and was gone.

⁂

Sure enough, the old woman had been right. Ben and Forrest got the appointment. Ben could not have been happier; he could not thank the Lord enough for this major blessing He had bestowed upon him.

"Hallelujah," he shouted over and over. "Praise the Lord!"

Forrest still had trepidations about the whole thing: the way his father had pursued this appointment to a church that his mother had warned him against trying to acquire for so many years, how fervently his father had gone about trying to obtain the appointment, and how it had consumed his every waking hour.

The bad feeling in the pit of Forrest's stomach had grown worse despite all of his attempts to stop the negativity.

Ben would be praising the Lord for days to come for his latest blessing, a testament to the fact that God did, indeed, answer prayer. He had worn out his knees praying for this blessing, and he was so grateful that the Lord had seen fit to grant him his heart's desire.

Be careful what you ask for, because you just might get it.

The next few weeks took on a hectic pace, but Ben welcomed whatever came with his new position with open arms. He could have easily qualified for the happiest man on earth. To him, this was about as close as he was going to get to heaven on earth. How he had wanted this church. Against all odds, he had wanted it—even against his beloved, deceased wife's admonishment against it, he had wanted it.

And, now, he had it.

Chapter Four

The white, two-story antebellum mansion stood like a beacon against the clear blue skies. It was massive with an upper balcony that ran across the entire front of the house, supported by six columns that stood at attention, three on either side of the heavy double doors.

During mid-day, it was simply spectacular to watch the sun glisten off the gold trim that adorned the tops of those columns.

The rooms inside were spacious with high ceilings and eclectic furnishings that were a mixture of antique, French Provincial, and Italian, all carefully chosen by the upper-scale good sisters of First St. Marks.

The porch, that wrapped around three sides of the lower level of the house, was furnished with wrought iron benches positioned up against the walls, and chairs placed around glass-topped tables holding an array of flowers and plants. Huge urns filled with ferns and other plants hung from the ceiling. It was a grand structure.

Even the darkest of night could not hide its splendor.

It was seven o'clock in the evening on the fourth Saturday after Ben and Forrest had been chosen as the new pastoral team at First St. Marks. The powers-that-be at the church had made haste in planning the *Pastoral Welcoming Banquet* for the two men.

This special black-tie event was being held here at the mansion. The place had not been occupied since the deaths of the last pastor of First St. Marks and his wife eight months earlier.

Not only were the new ministers being feted here this evening, but this was also going to be their new home. The elder Reverend Thomas had chosen the house over the parsonage beside the church—much to the dismay of the younger Reverend Thomas who had tried desperately to talk the older man into taking the smaller place as the old woman had suggested. For some reason, that he could not explain, he believed her when she said it was *safer*.

He was not sure what she meant by safer. He knew the place had once been a thriving tobacco plantation where the owner had owned slaves. He had also heard that the church's last minister and his wife had been found dead on the premises, and that the deaths had been deemed a murder/suicide—the minister being the perpetrator.

Had that actually been the case?

The old woman had told him that she thought the preacher and his wife had been murdered. Did she know something others did not?

He also knew that one of the former members of First St. Marks had bought and declared the old plantation the new parsonage, but he thought the minister should have a choice. He had tried to reason with his father but to no avail. He had talked with the older man until they were both exhausted.

His father had won that argument, and here they were at the mansion, the plantation—a place that would constantly remind them of one of the darkest, one of the most horrible eras in the history of America.

This place that was going to be their new home.

"Good evening, Deacon and Mrs. Davis," the parking valet said as he opened the passenger door of the white Rolls Royce, the last car—he hoped—that would be coming to this prestigious affair that evening. It was nearly eight o'clock. The event started at seven. No one else would dare arrive an hour late to an affair of this magnitude but the great deacon himself.

The man had more power than God.

"Good evening, Troy," Mrs. Davis said as she gave the young man her hand and stepped out of the car onto the marble walkway. Her white beaded, fitted gown, accentuated by diamond earrings, a broach—and many rings that adorned her fingers, added to the gilt of the evening and the magnificent house that was the cause for the big celebration that evening.

Troy Meadows bowed slightly. "Good evening, Mrs. Davis. Have a good evening, ma'am."

She smiled at him. He was such a nice young man. He was going to be something someday. "Thank you. I shall."

Troy thought he should be inside enjoying himself, not out here parking cars. The Junior Deacons of the great First St. Marks Baptist Church were treated like flunkies. Did they really have to wait until the old ones died to become full-fledged Deacons and, thus, people of means who would be treated with respect? Could he wait that long? He had to, he guessed, if he wanted to become a deacon at First St. Marks—and that he did.

He did, indeed. That's why he had volunteered for this lowly, degrading, shameful job tonight. No, it wasn't really a job, because there was no pay—just tips. He would have a pretty good night, though. The big spenders were out this evening. Davis would probably tip him a fifty. With the many tens and the three twenties he had received so far, he would probably do well.

They tipped their no-life-yet wannabes good to make sure they felt better about being their flunkies, he guessed.

They were wrong about him though. He did not feel better about standing around outside, parking their cars, and kissing their behinds while they enjoyed themselves inside—with food and all. This was really not his style, but he guessed he could fake it for a few more years.

He would take his new girlfriend, the beautiful and focused Yvonne Ann Mansfield, out on the town with some of his proceeds from tonight.

He could not have made a better choice in girlfriends. She had her head on straight, just as he did. They both knew what they wanted and the roads to take to get to their destinations.

Yvonne was also the daughter of David Lewis Mansfield, the head of a major pharmaceutical company in New York—he had forgotten the name of the main drug it peddled. Yes, peddled was what he meant, because everybody knew that sometimes prescription drugs did as much harm to the human body as the illegal ones.

Troy had to think of new ways to try to impress the lady, because he had decided that he wanted her in his life permanently.

He was glad she had chosen Clarksville U.

"Because Daddy and I think it has the perfect curriculum for me," she told him one day while they were eating lunch in the school cafeteria.

"I'm glad the curriculum suits you and your daddy," he had responded.

He liked Yvonne a lot, and he was sure love would eventually come. He was going to push for a wedding right after they graduated from the university—mainly because *Daddy* was loaded, and he (Troy) might need help furthering and financing his career. He would be the best son-in-law for which the man could ever hope.

Yvonne was also a religious young lady. Although she attended another church while in town (her family was Methodist), he would eventually get her over to First St. Marks once they were married, and she was living here in Clarksville with him. Being the wife of a deacon (although a junior one at first) would surely be impressive to any Christian woman.

So, although what he was doing tonight was far beneath him and against all of his principles, he would make himself content with it. This was his way of saying, "I'm humble; I'm

Christ-like. I'll humble myself, be one of your flunkies, because, someday, I want to be one of you. Well, not just one of you but the leader."

He was kissing behinds, the great Deacon Davis's to be sure. He knew this, and did not like it one bit. However, he wanted to sit at the man's feet—so to speak—and learn all he could from him, snake that he was.

Oh, he had heard things—lots of things about the wonderful Mayor Gaston Davis. What a good, upstanding, Christian man he was, a deacon in his church, no less. But he wasn't just a deacon; he was chairman of the deacon board, and an outstanding member of the community that he governed.

The accolades went on and on.

And so did the other comments. Everybody knew that he was a shrewd business man. That he would stop at nothing to get what he wanted. That rules did not apply to him. That if you crossed him, you were doomed. And the worst of all: he was a womanizer.

Now that part, Troy did not want to believe. The man was married to the most beautiful woman that ever walked the earth. Why would he want to play around when he already had what any other man would give his right hand to have? Why the woman's beauty was tantamount to that of both Michelle Obama and Jackie Kennedy-Onassis. So why would Davis cheat on her? That he would never understand—if it were true, of course.

But, then, he had been told, and truly believed, that one can't judge a book by its cover.

Maybe there was something wrong with the woman. But he would be darned if he could see it.

Yes, he was a deacon-in-training. But how long would he have to wait? He was just eighteen, fresh out of high school and into his first year of college. But he was a believer. He would do what he had to do to get what he wanted, and he wanted to be just like Mayor slash Deacon Gaston Davis.

Power was what he wanted.

What was the point of doing anything if one could not be in control?

His mother always told him he had leadership qualities. Well, at least he was the head parking valet for the evening, so, technically, he was in control of parking. Not much, but that was a start.

Whatever, he would take it and play along with their game. He heard about things that were happening around First St. Marks. There was some heavy game-playing going on, and he was learning how to play. He also knew how to keep his mouth shut. Yes, he could play their games as long, or maybe even longer than most of them. After all he had more time on his side than they did, so he was certain he would be the last one standing.

"Hello, Troy, my boy," Deacon Davis said, as he fell in step beside his wife, his white tuxedo complementing the lady's attire—and the house, of course. He handed Troy the spare key to his car and a fifty-dollar bill.

Troy slid the bill into his pocket. He would make sure he was in place to bring the man's car back to him after the event.

I want his spot on the deacon board and his job. Since I've already got my wife picked out—and she looks just about as good as Mrs. Davis—I'll just concentrate on those two things. Or maybe I'll skip the mayoral stint, and go on to the White House. I'm smart, and I think I could do a better job of running this country than some of the past presidents, Troy thought as he looked after the elegantly dressed couple that was about to join the happy throng of people inside.

"The Lord must have been in an extra good mood when He created that woman," Troy whispered to himself. Davis was one lucky man. Mayor and head of the Deacon Board at First St. Marks, too—with a woman on his arm that made men, old and young, do double-takes whenever she entered a room—even the church house.

If just wishing was a sin, as he had been told, there were a lot of sinners at First St. Marks—all over town, or any place that woman went, Troy was sure.

Now that was power.

"The kind of power I'm going to have one day," Troy whispered to himself.

"Determination is the key," his mother always told him.

Well, he was determined. He would have that power. It was a promise he had made to himself, and he planned to keep it.

"Have you ever seen so much white in your life?" One of the other valets/Junior Deacons for the evening asked as he joined Troy beside the white Rolls.

"Yeah, I worked it two years ago when Reverend Simms moved in. I had just become a Junior Deacon."

"That one didn't last long, did he?"

"Nope," Troy said. He slid into the smooth, leather front seat of the Rolls, closed the door, and drove off, headed to the spot he had saved just a few yards away for the great deacon's car. After all, Davis was his biggest tipper, so he deserved special treatment, now didn't he?

He would see how that felt, too, someday—except he would probably tip some poor kid a hundred-dollar bill.

Chapter Five

The perfect couple, as they had been called many times: the beautiful ex-model and the tall, handsome, distinguished-looking, mayor.

She was in her early fifties, tall and slender and still moved with a model's long, confident stride. Neither the silver that was starting to invade her once auburn tresses, nor the tiny wrinkles that were forming around her eyes, could diminish the beauty of her magnificently sculptured face that was enhanced by an olive complexion and big, dark brown eyes.

Gaston Davis was in his mid-fifties and an ex-high school and college football star. He stood five feet eleven inches with lots of muscles.

"There's not one ounce of fat on my body," he always bragged and worked out at the gym every other day to keep his body that way. His voice was deep and rich—the end result of years of cultivation. He had an intelligent-looking, square-shaped face with an almost flat nose with nostrils that flared whenever he was angry.

Most of the time, Gaston Davis seemed to be a most pleasant, most congenial, and a most caring man. A façade?

Maybe. Maybe not. But, then, most of the time, things always went Gaston Davis' way, so why wouldn't he be pleasant, congenial, caring, or even the happiest man ever?

Needless to say, his passion for sports got him the attention of the girls by the droves in high school and college. But he also concentrated on his studies. Unlike other students who had no idea where they wanted to take their careers upon graduation from college, Gaston Davis knew exactly where he was going.

After graduating in the top ten of his class, he came out fighting for a position in the political arena. Once he got a foothold, there was no stopping him. That's when he became a manipulations expert with other people's lives. He ran for mayor of Clarksville, and got the position his first time out of the gate. It was rumored that he wanted one more term, and then his next stop was the White House.

Octavia Lane had married Gaston Burton Davis while he was still struggling on his rise to the top. His career had sped up considerably after she came into his life, however. Some say she charmed his career up the ladder.

When Gaston finally made mayor of Clarksville, Octavia assumed her position by her husband's side as first lady with all the grace and charm of any person of esteemed royalty.

Gaston Davis was indeed mayor of Clarksville, Arkansas, but when he was involved with functions concerning the church, he preferred to be called Deacon Davis.

Becoming a deacon at First St. Marks Baptist Church was one of the best political moves he had ever made. It had certainly helped him in his quest to become mayor two and one-half years earlier. After all, First St. Marks was the largest, the most prestigious, and the richest African American church in the county.

It had been the members of First St. Marks, with the help of Reverend Simms, the late pastor, that had put him in office. When his first term was up, he expected the church to help him get in for a second term.

With the new preacher on board, it should be a cinch.

With a nod from the pulpit, the people of First St. Marks would certainly vote for him again and spread the word to others in their communities, and just like the time before, he would be the victor at the end of the day.

By the time the next election rolled around, he expected their new minister to be completely involved. Davis and his committee would begin coaching him soon.

After his second term, he would be ready for his big move.

First St. Marks belonged to Gaston Davis and his constituents. They had owned it for the past ten years or so. That was when they had begun putting things in place for Gaston to step into his rightful place as mayor of Clarksville. The untimely death of their last pawn, the Reverent Marshall Simms, had not changed a thing.

Tonight's event would be a testimony to that.

He believed they had found their man, the perfect replacement, the perfect pastor, the perfect pawn. He could see the new reverend salivating when they told him he had the position. The man was greedy for money and power. He was greedy for what First St. Marks could give him, and he could have it all.

But he was going to have to dance for it.

Davis believed the Reverend Benjamin Thomas was going to be a really good dancer.

He was willing to bet on it.

Chapter Six

"This way," Sir. Joshua Townsend, the butler who had been hired especially for this occasion, said as he led Deacon and Mrs. Davis through the splendid hallway lined with fresh flowers that had been delivered earlier in the day.

Townsend had traveled these hallways many times when the others were here. Now they had called him back, but just for the evening—which suited him just fine. The place gave him the creeps.

He had been paid quite handsomely to keep his mouth shut about the goings-on around the mansion, and he had complied. His hush money had enabled him to hang up his butler's uniform and become a proper gentleman—for a while. Unfortunately, he had made a few bad decisions and had been forced to come out of his early retirement, thus his assignment tonight. He was doing all right, but he was happy to get a job every now and then.

What he was being paid tonight would carry him for the next month or two if he budgeted wisely. But he would have to begin looking for a full-time position soon. He shouldn't have a problem. He was the best at what he did, and working for

First St. Marks at this stately mansion for so many years, had certainly been a plus. It added great weight to his resume, and he had gotten a glowing recommendation from Deacon Davis.

Townsend and the Davises entered the elevator. Townsend punched the button for the second floor. In a few moments, they stepped out into the spacious, elaborately-decorated great room.

The room was filled to capacity with dignitaries of First St. Marks Missionary Baptist Church: the deacons and their wives, the trusties and their wives; the superintendent of the Sunday School and his wife; the president of the Missionary Society and her husband; the Minister of Music, the president of the choir, and their entourage; the president of the Pastor's Aide Committee and her husband; and some of the other members who gave generously to the financial upkeep of First St. Marks.

Oh, yes, and all of the members of First St. Marks' Mothers' Board were also invited—free of charge.

Davis would like nothing better than to run all of those old ladies into the nearest river, especially that meddling McDonald woman who called herself some kind of psychic. He was really getting tired of her meddling.

That group was a bunch of cantankerous old biddies, set in their ways, with no room for change. But . . . they were First St. Marks' elderly ladies, and some of them were living on fixed incomes. Catering to this group was a big plus. It showed compassion, love for your fellow man—women in this case. It made Deacon Davis, and his group, look good; it made First St. Marks look good when people learned that it took good care of its seniors. The cost of a few dinners was all it took to create that image.

It was a good business move. He guessed the old hens were good for something.

Some of them paid their tithes; others gave pretty generously. But they just could not get all of them to tithe even when they were threatened with hell, fire and brimstone and accused of robbing God.

"Pulling out the *"bully stick"* as some of them called it.

Davis and his men would keep working on them and all of the other slackers at First St. Marks.

Davis needed his next term financed, and he was already preparing for his run for the White House. He expected First St. Marks to make a generous donation to his campaign. The ten percent he was already taking off the top of the Sunday morning offerings just wasn't enough—unless they got everybody involved in really giving, he was going to have to raise his percentage. The others could still make due with the three percent they pocketed. Then there was the auditor . . . the man was a drunkard and a womanizer. If he remained sober long enough to keep his job, and if some irate husband did not catch him in a compromising position with his wife and kill him, he would be content with his yearly ten-thousand-dollar bonus (hush-money really) and they would remain safe.

Of course, he had seen to it that many of the city officials and other dignitaries were invited to join them at this special occasion. He was on a mission to lure the city's most influential citizens to First St. Marks, and expected the Rite Reverend Benjamin Thomas to help him do that.

He smiled. His future was looking brighter by the minute.

The Reverend just needs a little grooming, Davis thought.

All of these people were gathered tonight to help the guests of honor, the new minister and his son, celebrate their new appointment.

He had heard the younger Thomas was bringing a date; the older minister had the good sense not to bring anyone with him. But extra food had been prepared, of course. There were always a few people who waited until the last minute to R.S.V.P, and unthinking people who brought extra guests without R.S.V.P.'ing for them. Or, maybe the younger Thomas had said he was bringing a guest, and someone on the committee had not recorded it.

Those who were not able to attend tonight's function had been excluded, of course. After all, such a prestigious affair should be attended by only the purest—no, that sounded more like a fascist statement—maybe *best* would be a better word. The best First St. Marks had to offer. That's why dinner was five hundred dollars a plate, and the dress code was strictly formal. He and his men were weeding undesirables out of all the controlling organizations at the church, and were replacing them with people who knew how to follow the rules, and, of course, those who paid their tithes and offerings.

For functions like the one tonight, all the powers-that-be at First St. Marks had to do was price the event out of the financial range of the undesirables; telling them it was sometimes necessary in order to raise the money needed to do whatever was needed around the church.

Some people believed anything they were told. God bless them.

First St. Marks was not a church for poor people, but as a church, it was obligated to accept all who came.

A pity, in Davis's estimation.

But they would tolerate the misfits and bleed them for every penny they could squeeze out of them.

Chapter Seven

"There they are," Evelyn Miles, a stout, dark-skinned woman, whose hair needed another coat of dye—if she wanted all of it to be of the same hue—said. She turned to her husband, John, a short, rotund man with a cowlick on the top of his otherwise bald head, a highball at his lips. "Late as usual. Octavia has to always make an entrance."

"She got your attention, didn't she? She looks really nice. That's some dress she's wearing," Deacon Miles said then downed his drink, and marched off to the bar to get another, his third—already.

"Dinner is served!" came the call for which this group of elite guests had been waiting all evening. This announcement was delivered by Sir. Joshua Townsend, who the First St. Marks executive board (made up of the church Deacons and Trusties) had hired to head up the household staff at the Lizzie Cochran Mansion (named after one of the founding members of the Church, now deceased) when the mansion—an old plantation really, with everything left in-tact, even the servants' quarters out back--was first opened. And, yes, he was back tonight to spearhead this special occasion.

The board had yet to decide how they would staff the house for the new ministerial staff, as the new pastors had chosen the mansion instead of the parsonage, as Deacon Davis knew without a doubt that they would. He didn't think they should be as elaborate with the staff as they had in the past. The least people they put out there, the better. It would be safer that way.

Mrs. Cochran had bought the house and donated it to the church for an alternate parsonage. The old five-room parsonage next to the church had stood empty since the generous donation twelve years earlier. The pastor then, the Rite Reverend Leon Williams, had jumped at the chance to move out of the parsonage at once. His wife and three teen-age children were in total agreement.

"It's truly a blessing," Mrs. Ruth Williams, First St. Marks' First Lady, had said.

"It sure is!" the children, Victor, Carl, and Marsha said, almost in unison. Some of the other children from the church had shown them the house, and what they saw, if only from a distance, had thoroughly impressed them.

Victor was delighted. "We can each have our own room!" He was tired of sharing a bed with his younger brother, Carl, who was an outrageously rough sleeper. Many nights, Victor had to run for his life and ended up sleeping on the sofa in the small living room. (Everything about the parsonage was small.) Victor, for one, could not wait to move into the mansion, and he could not wait for his friends to come over to visit, so he could show them the inside of the house that they had all just seen from the outside.

The Williams family was moving on up.

"Who wouldn't accept such a wonderful gift," Reverend Williams had said. Given the choice of continuing to stay in the parsonage or move into the mansion required no discussion or time to consider. It was a done deal as far as he and his family were concerned.

The staff that had attended Reverend Williams and his family and his successor, the late Reverend Marshall Simms and his wife, had packed up and simply disappeared after Reverend Simms' wife had been found floating in the pond out back and the Reverend himself had apparently committed suicide—all except Sir. Joshua Townsend, the butler. He had stayed.

It was a Labor Day weekend, and all the staff members had been given the weekend off—except for Sir. Joshua Townsend. Townsend had received a phone call around ten o'clock the morning of the incident. He had left shortly afterwards, and had returned three hours later as directed.

Upon his return to the plantation, he called the deacons and the police—in that order.

The deacons got there first, as planned. The police arrived a few minutes later and began questioning Townsend.

He told them he had found the Reverend Simms just as he was when they (the police) arrived: with a rope around his neck, hanging from the hanging tree out back in front of the servant's quarters, an overturned free-standing ladder on the ground beneath him.

After viewing the hanging scene, the police had searched the property, finding Mrs. Simms floating in the pond.

No, Townsend did not know what had happened. He had been away at the time. He had gone into town to get a few grocery items for Mrs. Simms. No nothing had seemed amiss when he left. Reverend and Mrs. Simms had been in the dining room finishing up breakfast, and Mrs. Simms was making plans for dinner.

Yes, since the cook was off for the week-end, Mrs. Simms was going to make dinner herself. She loved to cook and seemed to relish the times she had the chance. She and Reverend Simms were planning a quiet dinner at home instead of going out as they usually did on holiday weekends.

Yes, it had taken him a while to find all the things Mrs. Simms needed, because some of the major super markets were closed because of the holiday. Yes, he could show them what he had bought. And he did. He had actually gone shopping and produced a bag that contained several jars of various spices, barbeque sauce, two cans of baked beans, a cabbage, and a package of whole-wheat dinner rolls.

Yes, the Reverend and his wife had been having problems. Yes, Mrs. Simms wanted to leave the church, but Reverend Simms wanted to stay. Yes, he had heard them arguing many times. No, he did not know if the Reverend had been having an affair with some other woman at the church.

The questioning went on and on, and Sir. Joshua Townsend was ready with perfect answers for all of them. Most of his answers to most of the questions were lies, but Townsend had to follow orders, and Deacon Davis and his entourage were standing right there to see that he did.

His story and answers to the intense inquiry had satisfied the authorities. The case was ruled a murder/suicide: Reverend Simms the perpetrator.

A week later, the butler's bank account grew tremendously.

❧

"You just made it," Evelyn Miles said to Octavia Davis as she passed the Davises on the way to the bar to fetch her husband. She flashed the plastic smile she had been wearing all evening in the general direction of the mayor's wife.

"We knew they would wait," Octavia said, but was not sure the other woman had heard in her haste to get to her drunken husband.

Evelyn Miles retrieved her husband from the bar, and they went in search of their place cards at one of the long elegantly prepared tables. Deacon and Mrs. Gaston Davis did not have to hunt for their place cards. They went straight to the head table. Tonight, the Davises would be seated to the right of Reverend Benjamin Thomas.

After all, was not the chairman of the Deacon Board always the preacher's right-hand man?

Chapter Eight

"It's beautiful up here, isn't it?" Sylvia Madden's eyes were focused on the lighted, sprawling gardens below. Her arm was about the waist of the younger Reverend Thomas. She had finally gotten him alone, away from the crowd, if only out onto the terrace of the magnificent structure.

Sylvia's head barely reached Forrest's shoulder, even in her three-inch heels. She was five feet three inches tall and just a bit overweight.

"Just right," Forrest always told her.

She wondered. If she were just right, then what was the problem? Why was she still a single woman and hoping? Why wasn't she already Mrs. Forrest Thomas? Why were they waiting? No, why was he waiting? If it were left up to her, she would already be Mrs. Forrest Thomas, his wife.

She was more than ready to begin their life together.

And her parents were pushing her, especially her mother. Sometimes she wanted to tell them to stay out of her business, but, of course, she could not do that.

They only wanted what was best for her, their only daughter.

"We just want to know that you are secure in life, just in case something happens to us," her father told her.

"And we want to get to know our grandchildren," her mother had added with a wide smile on her face.

She did want children, and so did Forrest. But her mother was right. They needed to get started. They were both in their thirties, for God's sake.

Maybe . . . maybe she should start watching her diet. He said she was just right for him, but men often said things they really did not mean.

But he had asked her to marry him, and that showed her that, out of all the women he could have had, he had chosen her, so she guessed he did love her. And maybe she was just right for him after all.

She would make him a good wife. They would be good together. Didn't he know that? Didn't he know that the sooner they were married, the sooner they could begin their new life together?

The perfect life.

She wanted this man. She had for years.

They had taken the first step, but that was not enough. They had to at least set a date. Despite what he said, she was going to fix the weight thing. She was determined to get her weight back down to her usual one hundred and twenty pounds. Even her face looked fat.

She knew what it was: too much ice cream. But she loved the stuff. That and the two Pepsis she drank everyday that were the cause of the pimples on her face. She would have to correct that habit, too.

Her hair was her main asset. It hung halfway down her back and was naturally curly. Her hair and her high cheekbones, she had inherited from her paternal grandmother, Martha, who was half Cheyenne. "Any woman can make herself as attractive as she wants," Grandma Martha always told her.

She believed her grandmother. She just had to work harder at it.

Grandma Martha also told her to always be proud of herself and her Indian heritage.

And she was.

Forrest seemed proud of her Indian heritage, also. "My little Indian princess," he called her sometimes.

She was sure Grandma Martha would have approved of him, but she had died thirteen years earlier, leaving a void in Sylvia's life that Sylvia knew could never be filled.

Now that Forrest was going to be a rich man—or living like one anyway—and a good-looking man that was also a minister, women were going to be falling all over him. Preachers drew women like magnets, and some women would do most anything to get next to them.

There were a lot of women in that new church, and she wasn't sure her man was going to be able to resist the onslaught she knew was inevitable.

When they got married, she was moving her membership to First St. Marks right away. Oh, they were engaged, and she was wearing his ring, but she knew that, nowadays, a ring on a woman's finger did not mean a hill of beans to some women who were on the prowl.

Even a marriage license did not mean a thing to some women.

She really did not think she had anything to worry about though. She knew she could trust Forrest. He was a good man, a good Christian man. But she was tired of his excuses. She was ready to become his wife. She did not want to wait any longer. They had to take that next step, and she would just have to take her chances with the other women.

She had not expected their lives to take such a turn. He had talked about the great First St. Marks Baptist Church, but she never really expected him and his father to actually become the pastors. Not in a million years. She thought it had all been just talk. If she had only known.

She had work to do.

Dr. Mildred Dumàs

Forrest knew why Sylvia had maneuvered him out onto the terrace, away from the others. He loved her. He really did. He was thirty-five years old. It was time for him to get married, settle down, and have children. But he had to wait and see if this whole thing here at First St. Marks was just a dream or reality — although tonight had just about sealed things, he assumed.

His father had accepted the post of the new minister at First St. Marks, and he had signed on to be assistant pastor. There were four other associate ministers at the church, but he knew his father expected him to be "his second voice" as he called it — right beside him in every respect. His father had told the Pulpit Committee that they came as a package deal.

"What's going to happen to us, Forrest?" Sylvia asked, her voice suddenly taking on a serious tone.

"What do you mean?" he asked playing dumb. He knew exactly what she meant.

"You know what I mean," she said. "I want a commitment from you — tonight."

"I need more time, Sylvia," he said.

"You've had four years. Your excuse isn't valid anymore. You can not only afford a wife now, but just look at this mansion where you and your father are going to be living. It's so huge, we could have ten children and still have room for more."

They both laughed.

"These people are so gracious. I've never seen anything like it," she continued, sliding her arms about his neck. "Forrest, you've finally arrived. We could be so happy here."

They had been engaged two of the four years they had been seeing each other. They had pledged their love for each other. He had asked her to marry him, and the next day they had gone shopping for an engagement ring. It had not cost much, but it was pretty. Her love for him had superseded the cost of the ring, and she wore it with pride.

He told her at that time that they would have to wait to be married because he was not yet financially able to take care of a wife properly. He wanted everything to be just right: a

---

home of their own, money in the bank, and he wanted her to have the privilege of not having to work. He wanted her to be a stay-at-home wife. He wanted her to take care of their children and enjoy being a married woman. He wanted to be the only breadwinner, as a proper husband should.

She had agreed.

But now that had all changed. They could trade the ring for a more appropriate one, and, of course, the house situation would be solved, with just him and his father living here at the mansion. What a privilege it would be to be mistress of such a place. She could see herself redecorating—much like Jackie Kennedy had done when she became America's First Lady. She hoped she would not have a problem with the older ladies of the church who probably wanted things at the mansion to remain the same.

After all, since she was going to be the lady of the house, it should really be her choice, shouldn't it?

This would be their White House, their sanctuary, a place befitting a First Lady of a church.

Well, she was not a First Lady, yet, but it was certainly in the making. Forrest would not always be his father's second-in-command—or she hoped not anyway. Surely some church would recognize his brilliance as a minister and seek him out to be a full-fledged pastor in his own right—one of the mega churches, perhaps.

Now that would really be something.

In the meantime, being his father's assistant at First St. Marks and staying here at the mansion would do just fine.

She was glad she had not taken her mother's advice and broken off the engagement.

"Tell the deadbeat goodbye," her mother had said so many times.

Patience had finally paid off for her. After all, she had been told all of her life that patience was a virtue.

Dr. Mildred Dumàs

"There you two are. I've been looking all over for you. They're waiting for us at dinner, Son," Benjamin said, moving out onto the terrace.

"Thanks, Dad," Forrest said. *Right on time,* he thought. *But I love this woman, so why am I still stalling?* He wondered to himself. *Because there is just too much going on right now,* he thought.

Forrest took Sylvia's hand. "Come on, let's go have dinner then we can talk further. We'll set a date tomorrow," Forrest whispered in Sylvia's ear as they followed his father to their table.

"Why not tonight?" she whispered back.

"Because I'm sure they're going to have my father and me cornered for the rest of the evening."

Chapter Nine

Sylvia sat to Forrest's left. She loved the position. As temporary as it was at the moment, it was still a good feeling, and she could not wait to make it a permanent one. But she did not know how to fight whatever was happening with him. How could she fight the unknown? She had to find out what it was that had him so uptight.

And Forrest had been right.

At dinner, he and his father were feted and called upon to say a few words to the people who had chosen them to be their new leaders at First St. Marks.

The older Thomas happily obliged. He thanked his new flock profusely. "I can't find the words to thank you enough for your faith in me and my son. This appointment means the world to me. You have my undying gratitude, respect, loyalty, and love. I promise to serve First St. Marks with all the fervor and vigor the good Lord will allow. And the house . . ." He had to stop and compose himself for a moment, and then he continued. "I've never seen, nor ever heard of such a parsonage as this. In my wildest dreams, I would never have envisioned that I would be living in such a place. But, as all of you know, being the good Christian people that you are, that we can never underestimate our God. He looks after His own. He showers blessings upon those of us who have chosen to follow Him, sometimes blessings we don't have the capacity to even imagine. Oh, my brothers and sisters, He does work in mysterious ways. Yes, he does. Tonight is testament to that fact. The Lord has truly blessed my son and me beyond the imaginable." He turned and looked at his son who sat expressionless, until he realized his father wanted him to corroborate what he had just said.

Forrest forced a weak smile and gave a slight nod of his head.

The elder Thomas, satisfied, turned back to the people who were now holding his life in their hands and continued. "We are so grateful. God bless all of you for your generosity and your trust." He waved a hand through the air and prepared to sit.

Deacon Davis grabbed him by the arm. "Oh, don't sit back down just yet, Reverend. We're not through. Are we First St. Marks?" Deacon Davis looked out over the assemblage gathered for this grand event.

"We don't think so," said, Deacon Miles. He stood, dangling a key over his head. This is the key to your new automobile, Reverend Benjamin." He turned to Forrest. "Reverend Forrest."

Forrest looked on in disbelief; Ben wiped at his eyes.

Deacon Miles continued. "There's a brand-new Mercedes-Maybach Luxury Sedan sitting in your garage. We don't have a problem with the Cadillac you're driving now, but it is five years old. That can be your second car, but we want our new pastors to ride in style whenever you're representing First St. Marks."

The assemblage applauded profusely. Ben looked over the crowd that was applauding him with tears of gratitude in his eyes. He could not believe what was happening to him. It was all so unbelievable, so beyond anything he could have imagined.

God was really working in his life.

"You and your son can work out your schedule, and decide who gets to drive the new car when and where. Just promise there will be no fighting over it," Deacon Davis chimed in.

There was laughter throughout the room.

Mother McDonald, who sat near the back of the room at the table that had been designated for the mothers of First St. Marks bowed her head and said a silent prayer.

Deacon Davis took the key from Deacon Miles and handed it to Ben.

Ben wiped at his eyes, took the key and closed his hand tightly around it. "Thank you. Thank you. Thank you. I just don't know what to say." He waved a hand through the air, and then sat back down at the table.

He was thoroughly overcome with gratitude.

Forrest looked at his father, a concerned expression on his face.

"You just said it, Reverend. And you are welcome. We take good care of our pastors at First St. Marks," Deacon Davis said, a smile plastered on his face. He turned to Forrest. "Reverend Forrest . . ."

Forrest rose. What could he say? He certainly did not share his father's enthusiasm about their new appointment and the generous perks that had been added tonight. It all sounded good.

Too good perhaps?

Or, maybe his worries were unfounded. Maybe First St. Marks was a blessing after all. Maybe his mother had been wrong.

He realized that everyone was looking at him, expecting comments as the Assistant Pastor. He forced a smile. "Like my father, I am overwhelmed at your generosity and at the way you have welcomed us into the fold at First St. Marks. I am so grateful. As my father's assistant, I shall strive to serve the church in an upright, Christian, and God-fearing manner. Thank you." He smiled and sat back down at the table.

The assemblage applauded him, but not as vigorously as they had his father. After all, he was just the Assistant Pastor, and his acceptance speech had been quite short.

Too short for some.

And he did not seem as excited as he should have been after being hired as Assistant Pastor, given a mansion in which to live as long as he was the Assistant Pastor at First St. Marks, and a new car to boot.

Was he really grateful or was he just saying the words?

Sylvia beamed at her husband-to-be, and touched his hand as he sat back down beside her at the table. This was truly the most exciting night of her life. She could not wait for her and Forrest to be married, so she could share in his and his father's good fortune.

Despite Forrest's stated good intentions, he could not quell his skepticism about the church. Nor could he quell the uncanny urge he had to run as fast and as far as he could away from this fine appointment, the new car, and his and his father's fancy new residence.

The house was impressive, yes it was. It was one of the most beautiful homes he had ever seen. He should be overwhelmed with gratitude like his father, he guessed. But, to tell the truth, the place scared him. It was going to be his new home, and he was scared that it was also going to be the undoing of him and his father.

After dinner, the Reverends Benjamin and Forrest Thomas stood in a reception line to receive the well wishes of the elites, the people who really mattered, from First St. Marks Missionary Baptist Church—and, of course, the members of the Mothers' Board.

Then they were given a grand tour of the estate and told its history.

They learned about the late Miss Lizzie Cochran and her generosity. How she had made her fortune in real estate, following in her ancestors' footsteps. How her grandfather, and other members of her family, had been slaves in the 1800s on this very plantation. Her grandfather had been given a plot of land after his owner freed him, and he had built houses on that land and rented them to other freed slaves. How his son, Lizzie's father, had continued to buy land and build after her grandfather died, and how she had continued the real estate business until her death ten years earlier at the age of one hundred and thirteen.

Lizzie never married. "They're just after my money," she would say about the many suitors she had rejected along the way, and she had no children. Therefore, since she had no family to whom to pass the business and her money, she had left all of her worldly possessions to First St. Marks.

Miss Lizzie, as she was called by the congregation of First St. Marks, had bought the mansion because of its historical significance and because it had been the birthplace of members of her own family.

It was a horrible time in her family members' lives, so preserving the mansion was not something of which to be proud, but it was history. It was American history, and she believed the preservation of this place could tell the story of that dreadful era better than any book that could ever be written—although there were pamphlets, newspaper clippings, and probably a book or two that were in the making about the place.

But seeing the actual place where the most horrid, and brutal acts of man upon man had been committed was a visual that no one could ever forget.

The mansion was once one of Clarksville's many thriving plantations that had been owned by a Mr. Sam Witherspoon, a wealthy white man, who had no qualms about owning houses, land, cattle and people.

Miss Lizzie had been told by her father, who had been told by his father of the horrific conditions in which her family members had to live. She was told of the separating of her family members. How they had been sold away from one another, and how, once they were freed, they had searched the country trying to put the family back together. He told her how they had found some but not others, and how their hearts never mended, because of the loss of those family members. She was told of the merciless beatings and the hanging tree where family members had watched as other members of the family were hanged because of one thing or another.

Miss Lizzie had left the servants' quarters with the hanging tree out front just the way it had been when Mr. Witherspoon had owned the land, because she wanted everyone who so desired to experience the horrors it represented, the horrors of slavery: the most inhumane practice of human sacrifice, bondage, destruction, degradation, and barbarism ever known to man—her exact words, they were told.

"Our people—slaves," said Deacon Miles. "My great grandfather, his mother, his father, two brothers and three sisters all lived and worked all of their lives on a plantation similar to this one in the great state of Mississippi."

The accounts went on and on. How the slaves' blood had fertilized the land, making it the rich soil it was today. How those poor men and women, boys and girls, were still working on the Witherspoon plantation today—their blood helping to grow the beautiful flowers in the flower beds, the grass, the trees . . . How the church board had agreed with Miss Lizzie that it would be the perfect place to house their pastors and their families as they came and went.

They wanted the head of their church to have better than the small parsonage adjacent to the church; that living in an historical monument—as bad as its history might have been— was a special gift, indeed.

The church had its annual picnic at the plantation that included a tour of the house and grounds with the church historian as the tour guide narrating the history of the place—as stipulated in Miss Lizzie's will.

"The children need to know their history," she said. "And because of the miseducation of our people, we are the ones who are going to have to teach them."

And out here in the country, away from the church, the ministers would be much easier to control, Deacon Davis thought.

After the tour of the house and a portion of the grounds, where light permitted, the two men were surrounded by one group after another, everyone trying to find out all they could about their new pastor and his assistant.

Ben and Forrest were subjected to questions and idle conversation until well after midnight when Deacon Davis announced that the event was over for the evening.

"Go home, and get a good night's sleep, so you can get up early enough to make it to Sunday School in the morning."

"Correction," Deacon Miles said. "He means this morning."

Everybody had a good laugh, and then went their separate ways to their various homes.

Deacon Davis and a few others knew all they wanted to know about their new pastor. The Pulpit Search Committee had done a thorough background check on Benjamin Thomas months before they asked him and his son to consider taking the appointment at First St. Marks.

After the church's last pastor's sudden death, they had waited a while before soliciting a new pastor, allowing Reverend Simms' assistant, Reverend Matthews, to carry on—knowing all the while they had to get rid of the man, because he, like Simms, was determined to "clean up things around First St. Marks," as he put it.

Cleaning up things around First St. Marks was a deadly thing about which to even think. The Rite Reverend Matthews had been warned, but he chose to not heed that warning, so he could not be allowed to stay. He had waged a good battle, but in the end, there was just no other solution.

He had been allowed to stay as long as he did because of the embarrassing circumstances that surrounded Reverend and Mrs. Simms' deaths.

Although the mayor, and others in high places had tried to keep the incident out of the papers, it still leaked out to the public. *Mysterious Deaths at the First St. Marks Pastor's Parsonage,* the article began and went on to tell all the gory details, embellishments and all, about the incident.

Deacon Davis was sure The Rite Rev. Thomas had also heard of the scandal surrounding First St. Marks, but he was apparently smart enough not to mention it. Davis liked that. As long as the man knew how to play the game, they would get along just fine.

The church community had bowed its head in shame long enough. It was now time to move on. And they had their new pawn. Davis was sure he had recommended the right man.

All the Reverend Thomas had to do was follow orders. His main functions would be to keep the parishioners in a giving frame of mind and campaign for him (Davis) from the pulpit.

The Reverend Simms had been so good at both—at first. It was a shame he had awakened one morning with a new-found religion that told him what he was doing was wrong, that the church was being bilked, and he had to put a stop to it. He had talked it over with his wife, and she had agreed.

His mistake was to approach Deacon Davis and his Clan with his intentions.

What had happened to him and his wife was a shame.

They would be missed.

Chapter Ten

Forrest drove Sylvia home in the new Mercedes that the church had presented to his father during the ceremony that evening.

"You're the first to drive it, son. It's as much yours as it is mine. We're a team," the older man said, handing Forrest the key to his latest gift from this most generous church he was now pastoring.

"What a blessing this church is to us! Hallelujah!"

His father was still praising the Lord for their new assignment and all the perks that were coming with it. Forrest had to admit that the house and the car—and the money, of course—were most generous and welcomed, but he still had a bad feeling about it all. His mind kept telling him that this latest piece of luxury from the powers-that-be of First St. Marks Baptist Church was not the blessing his father seemed to think it was.

He could not shake the feeling.

Why? Why were they being so generous? Was this normal for First St. Marks? Was this normal for any church for that matter?

He wondered.

But, then, he guessed it was. Some churches, the mega ones anyway, did not just purchase their pastors new, fancy cars like the Mercedes he was now driving, but they also purchased jet planes for them. He heard that one such minister, whose church had already bought him one jet had the nerve to ask his congregation to dig deep into their pockets to purchase him another.

Forest guessed the old one had gotten too slow for him.

He smiled. *This is a fast world now-a-days,* he thought.

But he couldn't help but think that all these wonderful things that were happening to him and his father were just coming too fast. Maybe they were legitimate, and maybe they were not. But if Deacon Davis and the other officials of First St. Marks had some phony agenda, they certainly know how to bait their trap, because *his* father was eating right out of their hands.

But as far as his father's situation was concerned, he needed to have a nice, long conversation with the Lord.

❧

Forrest and Sylvia had thoroughly enjoyed the smooth, luxurious ride to her parent's house.

He walked her to the front door, kissed her, said goodnight, and then turned to leave.

"Why don't you come in for a few minutes? Wind down with a cup of coffee," she suggested.

"I can't, Honey. It's late, and I have to get back just in case my dad's still up working on his sermon. He always bounces things off me. He always says, *two heads are better than one.*"

"Okay . . ." she said, disappointment coming through, loud and clear, in her tone.

He didn't dare go into the house for fear she would bring up the subject of marriage again.

He had to have more time to think things through. He had to have a clear head when making major decisions like getting married, and right now his head was full of so many other things, unexpected things, things that just kept popping up, things that should have been welcomed, graciously received, and counted as blessings. But that was not the case with him, and he could not understand why. With so many things clouding his mind, he could not concentrate on his impending wedding.

Marriage would be a life-time agreement for him. When he made that vow, he planned to keep it.

"Yeah, I'll call you," he said, and hurried on down the steps, then down the sidewalk to the curb where the impressive Mercedes-Maybach awaited him. When he got into the car, he smiled, waved at her, and then drove off down the street.

Forrest's thoughts raced on as he drove back to the mansion? Plantation? He wasn't sure what he should call the place.

Deacon Davis was deep in thought on his ride back to his home—nothing short of a mansion, also—after the big bash at the Cochran Mansion for his two new pastors.

Yes, the trap was set, and the Reverends Thomas and Thomas, father and son, were falling right into it.

He smiled.

Chapter Eleven

"Lead us not into temptation... Luke Chapter 11, verse 4," Forrest said out loud as he pulled the new Mercedes into the three-car garage. Sometimes the temptation was so great, it was hard trying to live by the word.

He hoped his father was doing the right thing.

The new car drove like a breeze, and the house, no the mansion, was wonderful. He could get used to living like. . . maybe royalty here in America. He had to admit his family had never had such luxuries before. They had lived comfortably, he guessed, but this . . . this was beyond his wildest dreams. He and his father had been instantly catapulted into the lap of the kind of luxury to which they could easily become accustomed.

He could certainly see why his father had wanted this assignment so badly. He didn't think even he (his father) had envisioned the enormity of it all.

Maybe their ship had finally come in.

Forrest shook his head, bringing himself out of his reverie. "Not without a catch," he said out loud to himself. There had to be a catch, and he guessed it was left up to him to find out what that catch was. Somebody had to keep a level head. In this case, under the circumstances, he assumed that somebody would have to be him.

Forrest found his father still upstairs in the ballroom, standing in the middle of the floor, the same look of awe that had been on his face all evening, still there.

"I can't believe it, Son. I just can't believe all this is really mine."

"It belongs to the church, Dad."

"But that's mine, too, now."

"No, Dad, it's not."

"It's a miracle, Son! That's what it is. A miracle! Thank you, Lord! Thank you, Jesus!" Ben went on as if Forrest had not spoken.

"Dad, I'm not so sure we're doing the right thing. We might be deluding ourselves. I'm having doubts about what I see happening here."

"God moves in mysterious ways, Son."

"Dad, I don't know. I just don't know about all this. It's too much too soon. I think. If Mother were still alive—"

"But she's not," Ben interrupted, the words coming too quickly from his mouth. He did not want to think about his dead wife now. She was a part of his past. He had to live in the present, and that included his new appointment at First St. Marks. His dream had finally come true. He had the church he had wanted for years.

It was his. It was his--and all the perks that came with it.

"She's dead, Son. Gone from us forever. She had a problem with First St. Marks. I didn't. I could see the potential. She could not. I don't mean to be abrupt or disrespectful of her feelings, but I have to do what is best for me."

He looked at his son, his eyes pleading. "Son, we've paid our dues, and now the Lord is blessing us. This is our Eden, Forrest. The White folk have had their Edens all over the world for years. Why, this very place was once a White man's Eden. Look how the hands of time have reversed that now. We, the people who were once relegated to the slave quarters out back, and were only permitted in the big house—this house, through the back door, no less—whenever the master saw fit, now own the big house and everything around it. This is history in the making, and we're part of it."

"Dad—" Forrest began, his voice concerned.

"This is ours, Son. All ours." Ben said interrupting him again. He looked about, marveling at his magnificent surroundings. He raised his arms, closed his eyes, and his voice boomed as it did when he was winding down his sermons on Sunday mornings, bringing his point home, sending the good sisters into the arms of the Lord for a brief period of uncontrollable shaking, screaming and holy dancing. "This is our paradise on earth! This is our *Black Eden!*"

"Dad, don't I have some say in this? We need to talk."

"I'm tired, Son. I'm going to bed. I have to get up early to finish my sermon. I just hope I can sleep. This has been an evening I will never forget as long as I live." He looked toward the heavens and shouted, "Hallelujah!"

Forrest looked at his father, and what he saw in the older man's eyes scared him.

Chapter Twelve

The woman sat on the Mothers' Bench, the muscles in her face set in a stern, rebuffed manner. She stared at him, her gaze unwavering.

She had told him not to take the house, but he had not heeded her warning. Why should he deprive himself of all the wonderful things First St. Marks had to offer? He would not. He could not. He wanted it. All that had been given to him. He wanted it all.

He counted all of it a blessing.

The woman had seen the house, no the mansion? Who could refuse such a gift? He certainly could not. There was no comparison between that house and the little parsonage beside the church. No comparison at all, and he would not deprive himself because of some old woman's whim.

He would not, so she could stop all the frowning and staring at him.

He did not know what the woman's problem was, but he was not going to allow her to block his blessings. Not this blessing anyway. It had been too long coming, and now that it had come, he was going to latch onto it with all his might. He would be the best minister First St. Marks ever had.

She would see; they would all see. The Pastor's Search Committee would never regret assigning him to this post, and the parishioners would never regret having him as their new pastor, their new leader. He had never led such a vast congregation before, but he should not have any problems—and he had assistant pastors to help, including his son. Everything would just be on a bigger scale. He smiled.

He would just have to grow with his blessings.

His son . . . What was his problem with the blessings that had been bestowed upon them? He could not understand Forrest's reservations about having a nice home and a new car. He said he had thoroughly enjoyed driving the car the night before, and he admitted that the house was like no other he had ever seen or in which he could have ever hoped to live.

So, what was the problem?

Maybe he should suggest that the church rent the parsonage —very cheaply—to some needy family in the neighborhood, or in the church, for that matter. Maybe there was such a family in the church. Maybe such a gesture would vindicate him in the eyes of the old woman. Maybe he could ...

What was he thinking? He could not worry about what that woman thought of him. He had to do what was right for him. Didn't everybody? Preachers were only people, too. No, not exactly. They were men of the cloth, disciples, carriers of the word. But they had wants and needs just like everybody else, and he wanted and, yes, even needed what that wonderful house had to offer him and his son.

Yes, he had accepted the house, because that was what he wanted.

Nevertheless, he felt like a little boy who had disobeyed his mother.

He glanced back over at the woman. Her accusing eyes seemed to be boring right through him.

It was time for the sermon. He looked out into the congregation, rose, and went to the pulpit.

"Help us, today, Lord!" he shouted. "Shower us with your blessings in this place! This day! Hallelujah, saints! Hallelujah! Praise the Lord!"

"Hallelujah," came the response from some of the congregants.

"Thank you, Jesus," came another response from the direction of the Mothers' Bench.

Did he dare look? Could it be . . .? No. It was probably one of the other ladies. He didn't think she had forgiven him so soon. Not the way she had been glowering at him. Maybe some of the enthusiasm from the other mothers would rub off on her, and soon, he hoped.

Come on, ladies; help me out here, he thought.

"Help me, somebody. Help me praise the Lord this morning, God is still on the throne! Yes, he is! Please turn with me to . . ."

＜ᢒᎧᢒ＞

Ben preached on, but about the middle of his sermon, curiosity got the better of him. His eyes darted back to the woman, and he knew instantly that he had made a mistake. The intensity of her stare unnerved him so much he began to stammer, unable to take his eyes from her face. It was as if she had a drawing power, pulling on his senses, interrupting his train of thought, causing him to perform poorly.

He rambled on until he finally managed to wrench his eyes free. He picked up momentum, hacked a few times, trying to bring himself back, trying to evoke even a whisper of an "Amen" or a few more "Hallelujahs" or a "Yes, Lord," from somebody. Anybody.

He threw his head back and whooped. "Hear me now, saints! Hear me!"

"Preach, Reverend!" came a weak voice from his right.

"Tell the truth!" came another, this time from the left.

"Yes! Yes!" from somewhere in the congregation.

He was back. Thank the Lord.

Ben preached on for a few more minutes. The church warmed up to him—well as warm as First St. Marks was capable of getting, he supposed. The place was definitely too quiet for his taste, but he would learn to live with it. Yes, he would. Sometimes one had to adjust, especially if it was worth one's while, and First St. Marks was certainly worth his while, and then some.

He was about to begin living the good life—like some of those television evangelists: Clifford Downs, James Caldwell, and Maurice Towers. . . . Who knew? Maybe First St. Marks would decide that they wanted to make their new pastor a television evangelist, also. Now that would be something. You talking about coming into power—well, more power—that would be the utmost, his utopia. But, in the meantime, he would continue to thank the Lord for what he had now.

⁂

Ben finally closed his Bible and took his seat.

The pianist struck up a cord on the piano, the choir director motioned the choir to stand, and the choir began to sing a slow, dull song.

Forrest leaned close to his father's ear. "What happened up there, Dad?"

"That woman," Ben said wiping frenziedly at his face with his handkerchief.

"What woman?" Forrest asked.

"Over there on the Mothers' Bench." Ben gestured to his left. "I've got to talk to her. Tell her to stop."

"Stop what, Dad?"

The pianist hit a loud cord on the piano, and Forrest jumped to attention. They were waiting for him. It was time to open the doors of the church. It would be quite impressive if they could pull more new members into the fold so soon into their new assignment.

He would give it his best shot.

Forrest rose and went to the pulpit. "The doors of the church are open. Come, give your life to Jesus while you still have time. While the blood still runs warm in your veins. Tomorrow is not promised." He raised his arms in a welcoming gesture. "Come. Is there one? Give your life to Jesus."

There were four converts.

"Hallelujah!" Forrest and Ben shouted in unison.

"Praise the Lord!"

"Hallelujah!"

"Thank you, Jesus!"

The congregation of First St. Marks shouted and applauded for the new converts.

Ben went down to welcome and receive the new converts into the body of First St. Marks. The church was growing under his leadership, and that was always a good sign.

∼✑∼

The parishioners of St. Marks stopped to shake the ministers' hands and make brief comments. Some simply walked right past them without even acknowledging their presence—again. But this time, Ben felt safer than he had before, for he was now the pastor of this flock. If some did not like it, they could just move on as they were doing.

Then he saw her, the woman. She was coming toward them. Ben had an urge to turn and run. But, of course, his feet stayed planted to the spot where he stood. He had to face this woman and let her know that he was a grown man, her pastor, to be exact, and that he made his own decisions.

"You moved into the house. That was a mistake. A big mistake." She did not offer her hand. She simply prepared to move on.

Forrest caught her gently by the arm turning her back to face them. "What's your name, Sister?"

"I am Mother Lucynda McDonald. That place is cursed. No one can help you now. No one!" She attempted to pull free of Forrest's grasp.

Ben took her gently by the arm. "Why do you say the house is cursed, Mother McDonald? Please explain that to us."

"You should have listened. It's too late now." She eased her arm out of his grasp and moved on toward the front door.

An old man moved in front of them. He stuck out his hand, shaking hands with the father then the son. "Listen to her. She knows what she's talking about. She saved my wife's life and mine two years ago. You need to listen." The man began to move away.

Forrest caught him by the arm. "Wait, please! Uh, Brother . . ."

"Sheppard," the old man said. "Brother Jacob Sheppard."

"How did she save your lives, Brother Sheppard? Please, tell us," Forrest said.

"We were going to Hawaii for vacation. She told us she had seen something in a dream and that we should cancel our trip. My wife insisted that we do just that. I was mad as a wet hen, and I told her and my wife just that." He paused a moment, then continued. "The plane we were booked on went down ten miles outside of the airport."

Bro. Sheppard turned and walked away from his two new pastors. Ben and Forrest watched his exit, both of them speechless for a moment.

Then they turned back to bidding the congregation of First St. Marks a good day.

Chapter Thirteen

"Cursed? This house cursed? How can people actually believe such nonsense?" Ben was incredulous. He and Forrest sat at either end of the long dining table in the elaborate dining room of their new home, with its satin papered walls, silk-draped windows and elegant furnishings. The table was so long, they had to almost shout to be heard during a conversation.

Mrs. Connie Louise Barber, their housekeeper slash cook, had just finished serving the first course of their Sunday afternoon dinner: gazpacho, a cold vegetable soup.

"The perfect thing for a hot, sultry summer afternoon," Mrs. Barber said.

Perhaps it would have been if either of the men had liked gazpacho. They did not. It wasn't bad, really, but they preferred their soup hot. But they ate the gazpacho. After all, they were living like the rich and famous now, although they only had one person attending them in their new spacious home.

Ben had heard that the other ministers and their families had a cook, a housekeeper, and a butler. But maybe that was because some of the other ministers had families. Well, for whatever reason, they would just make themselves satisfied with Mrs. Barber. She was doing an excellent job. They only used a few of the rooms, so there was not much for her to do really.

When in Rome . . .

"Perhaps there is some truth to it, Dad." Forrest's face was pensive. He did not want to believe what the woman had said either, but his gut feeling told him there was something wrong somewhere. As hard as he tried, as hard as he prayed about it, he could not shake the feeling.

Something was desperately wrong.

Maybe they should move out of the house and take the parsonage beside the church as the old woman had told them to do in the first place. But he knew his father was so enamored with the mansion that trying to get him to move out on a "gut feeling" would undoubtedly be an impossible task.

"Son, please. That kind of thinking is a bit archaic, don't you think? We're not living in the dark ages anymore. We have evolved."

"I know, but I still can't help but think maybe we should have taken the parsonage."

Ben laughed. "And refuse all this?" He gestured about the room. "In a way, this is the church parsonage. It's the house the church members have chosen for their pastor and his family. That's us now, Son. We can't, in good conscience, give up this blessing the Lord has seen fit to bestow upon us. Now can we? Black Eden. It has a nice ring to it, don't you think, Son?"

What Forrest really thought, he was afraid to tell his father.

Chapter Fourteen

"June is so many months away. I don't want to wait that long. I really don't have to be a June bride. I just want to be your wife," Sylvia said.

"When then?" Forrest asked.

"I want to get married as soon as possible, in the next few months. We've been engaged for so long. I want to be your wife."

"Okay, maybe around Christmastime. A holiday wedding might be nice.

She beamed. "That would be wonderful. I'll go see Rev. Simpson and see what his calendar looks like."

"All right. You're going to make a beautiful bride whenever we decide."

"Thank you." She cuddled up closer to him.

They sat on the sofa in the living room of her parents' home in Edgemont, a little town about ten miles east of Rushmore, where the Reverends Thomas and Thomas had been pastor and assistant pastor at the Greater Rock Missionary Baptist Church before going to First St. Marks.

It was at Greater Rock that these two young people had met and fallen in love. Sylvia's eyes had been on the tall, lanky, and oh, so handsome, assistant pastor for a long time before he finally decided to ask her out for coffee.

They were leaving the church one evening after a long meeting about the children's upcoming Easter program.

Finally, Sylvia thought. She had been waiting for this moment for such a long time. She was beginning to think the young minister had his eyes on someone else. Just about every single woman in the church had her eyes on him; that was for sure, and he knew that. Not only the ones in their age range, but some of the middle-aged women, also.

It had become quite popular for older women to seek out younger men now-a-days, The Cougar era for women had been born.

Maybe payback for all the years older men had chosen younger women over women their own age?

Maybe.

But the Reverend Forrest Thomas had asked her out—if only for coffee—and Sylvia was so ecstatic, she could hardly contain herself.

She had convinced herself that that had been the best cup of coffee she had ever tasted.

But she could not get ahead of herself, because she did not know how many more cups of coffee he had bought before hers.

Maybe he was testing the field of women at his beck and call, the ladies-in-waiting. That's exactly what they were, and she was included in that number. She could not forget that fact.

The contest had been fierce: The sisters of Greater Rock dressing to the nines, getting into every organization at the church in which they thought Assistant Pastor Forrest would be involved so they could be seen—all literally throwing themselves at his feet.

Sylvia had done just the opposite. Oh, she dressed nicely and kept herself visible but in a subtle way. She was not jumping all over the place, flitting from one meeting or organization to another hoping Forrest would be there just to *be in his face.* That was not Sylvia's style. No, indeed.

Sylvia Rhonda Madden would never have been caught dead chasing a man—her grandmother's advice. And it had paid off for her.

She had been involved with the Children's Church before he came, and that was where she was going to stay. Working with children was her passion. She loved them and they loved her. It was a match made in Heaven, she always told herself. That was the only organization with which she was involved—other than singing in the "Bells of Greater Rock" Choir. (One of the former pastors of Greater Rock had given the choir that name, because he said they sounded like bells from Heaven.) They could sing, and she was proud to be a member of that great choir.

The choir and the Children's Church kept her busy.

That was enough.

Forrest had eventually been put in charge of the Children's Church, and it was there that they had connected. He was impressed with the way she had organized the department, the way the children looked up to her, the way she took so much pride in her work. He told her she looked so natural with children sitting at her feet when she read Bible verses to them.

It was there that she had not only captured his attention but his heart as well.

It was at Greater Rock that they had become engaged. The event they both had attended was a Box Supper given by the Missionary Society. One of the older sisters had introduced the society to this "ancient" (as the younger women called it) supper idea.

Each woman would prepare supper for two and arrange it in a decorated box. The ladies would stand in a row behind the curtain on the stage in the Fellowship Hall with only their toes showing. Each lady's box supper was placed to the right of her toes. Each man participating in the supper would pay a set price and take his turn selecting the pair of toes that intrigued him.

When all toes had been touched and Box Suppers gone, the woman who made the supper and the man who had touched her toes would sit and enjoy her supper together.

Dr. Mildred Dumàs

Sylvia had cooked all afternoon that day. She had been watching Forrest at the many luncheons and dinners the church had throughout the year and knew his favorite foods all too well.

She had been practicing at home, cooking for her man, as she had begun to call him, but only to herself. She was not silly enough to put herself in a position to be publicly humiliated by claiming the man prematurely.

"I'm glad to see you taking such an interest in cooking all of a sudden," her mother said.

She had always reminded Sylvia of the old cliché: *The way to a man's heart is through his stomach.*

Well, Sylvia was working on getting into this man's heart—real hard.

That night, Sylvia had worn an orange dress. Forrest had made sure he was as close to the front of the line as possible—praying all the while that no other man would touch his woman's toes. He had been in luck. He tapped the toes with the toenails painted a bright orange—their signal—and he and Sylvia had eaten her succulent southern fried chicken, potato salad, three-bean salad, butter-honey-biscuits, and apple-raisin pie.

Forrest had smacked his lips and told Sylvia how delicious her supper was. She had thanked him, trying hard, but not too successfully, not to blush.

All of this had not gone unnoticed. There were many jealous female eyes on the happy couple that evening.

Forrest was oblivious; Sylvia tried not to notice the stares.

Well, all is fair in love and war, she thought, a sly smile playing on her lips. They had cheated, but it had been worth it.

That night after he had taken her home, in the midst of watching TV and talking about the wonderful time they had had at the Box Supper, Forrest had gotten down on his knees and proposed to her. "It was the bean salad," he told her.

She had laughed, and said, "yes, yes, yes!"

She knew how much he liked her mother's famous bean salad. She had seen him scraping the bowl at a couple of other functions. Sylvia had perfected that dish especially for the Box Supper.

And it did the trick, she thought.

She chuckled. "Bean salad, huh?"

"Well, that and the fact that I'm crazy about you," Forrest said."

Thank you, Lord, she thought as she let her eyes drift upward. She had gotten her man. She smiled. "I love you, too."

But, now, she had to keep her man. She thought of all those other women who had been chasing him and shuddered. They would be so surprised when they heard that she and Forrest were engaged. Would they back off now?

She wondered.

Sylvia knew how desperate some women were. She knew how desperate she had been lately while waiting for Forrest to propose to her. Would she have backed off gracefully if the shoe were on the other foot?

Yes, she would have, because she would have to respect the man's decision to choose whatever woman he wanted. She would be forced to move on with her life, as painful as that might have been, without him. But her mother, her grandmother, and her father always told her that there were many fish in the sea that she was a beautiful, talented and desirable woman, and someday God was going to send the perfect man her way.

She believed them.

But he wanted her. He really wanted her, not some other woman.

But there is a shortage of men in this country, she thought. But she had trusted the Lord to send her a good man, and he had answered her prayer by giving her Forrest.

Those other women would just have to pray the same prayer and wait on the Lord.

Forrest is mine, she thought.

Forrest understood why Sylvia wanted to be married at Greater Rock. After all, she had not moved her membership yet.

"I'm going to wait until we're married, until I'm officially Mrs. Forrest Thomas," she told him.

So, they were going to make it official in a few months. He didn't know why, but Forest did not feel too excited about that. Not now when he was in such turmoil about the new life he and his father were about to enter into as pastor and assistant pastor of First St. Marks Baptist Church.

He could not shake the feeling that something was just not right.

"Your room at the mansion is perfect," Sylvia said, bringing Forrest out of his reverie. "We won't have to do a thing to it, and I can't wait to cook in that huge kitchen." Sylvia had her eyes closed envisioning herself as mistress of her future husband's new home and the wonderful life she was going to lead as the new Mrs. Forrest Thomas. She was elated! No, she was beyond elated; she was in heaven, right here on earth.

Thank you, Lord, she thought.

Forrest looked at his future wife. He had seen the same look that was on her face now on his father's face the night before.

Something inside his stomach moved.

Chapter Fifteen

Ben's name for their new residence caught on. Soon, the entire church community and others in the town of Clarksville were talking about "Black Eden."

Some liked the name and spoke of the place fondly.

Some could not forget the dark history the place harbored, however. The new name would do nothing to change what it was: a house of horror. It was no place for anyone to live, certainly not men of God. How could they hold on to their faith and do the work of the Lord the way they should with the residue of so much evil surrounding them?

The place should not have been bought and designated a parsonage for the church.

It should have been torn down—if for no other reason than to erase the place where so many horrible things happened. Miss Lizzie had been wrong to buy it and give it to the church, for the church parsonage, no less.

The woman must have been losing her mind in her old age.

There had been so many incidents, starting with the horrors of slavery—the many people who had been so brutally abused, sometimes unto death by their so-called masters and overseers—

Satan's disciples; that's what they were. Hanged on a tree until all the life was choked out of them—and she left the tree right there for all to see. Why?

Some of them just could not understand why anyone would want to do such a thing?

"Preserving the history," Miss Lizzie said. "How can one chart one's future without knowing one's past?" Or "One has to know where one has been in order to know where one is going." She was always coming up with some outlandish phrase or another. She was a smart woman, but couldn't she have found a better way to preserve history?

Just about everyone in town had toured the mansion, and most of them had even dragged their children along.

Oh, it was a sight to see, especially the slave quarters and the hanging tree out back. The adults left there as angry as anyone could be, and the children, confused. They just could not understand how such things that they had been told about the place could have happened. Here in America? It was an enigma all right, even to some of the adults, because it was all just too gruesome to even imagine. But it had happened. That was a part of our history, American history—not understandable, but true.

Even in this day and age, strange things continued to happen at that place.

There was the incident where Reverend Williams and his family had fled for their lives in the middle of the night, after the Lord had given Reverend Williams a dream that they were in danger if they stayed. At least that was the story that the members of First St. Marks, the police, and the newspapers had told.

Then there were the murders of Reverend Simms and his lovely wife that had shocked the town to its core. The townspeople did not believe the murder/suicide story. It was too far-fetched. Why would the minister kill his wife then himself? Why? It seemed no one could answer that question.

The people of Clarksville knew that both the minister and his wife had been murdered no matter what the police, those members of First St. Marks, and the newspapers said.

They just knew it.

There were just too many weird things happening at that house.

That place had a stigma attached to it. There just wasn't any good that could come from a place like that no matter how it had been spruced up to look like any other large imposing, multi-million-dollar residence, and given a new historic-sounding name.

Beautiful it was, but the ugliness that it harbored made it a sore thumb to the community.

There was something wrong with that house.

So, they would just wait and see what the future held for the new ministerial staff of the First St. Marks Missionary Baptist Church.

They just hoped nothing like what had happened to the other ministers and their families who had stayed at the mansion would befall the new ministers. They did not think First St. Marks could stand another catastrophe.

The community could not stand another catastrophe.

They would just have to keep praying the blood of Jesus over those ministers, and First St. Marks, too, for that matter.

And they would keep hoping that nice Pastor Williams and his family had left on their own as had been reported. But it was strange that they would leave without a word to anybody—and in the middle of the night like thieves.

From what were they running? What was happening at that church that had spilled over to that house?

God only knew.

They just hoped the Williams family wasn't buried on the grounds of that fancy place. But knowing the history of the Cochran Mansion—now Black Eden--they would not be surprised at anything that happened there.

Not a thing.

Maybe there should be an excavation of the grounds at that place. What would they find? Only the good Lord above knew.

That place gave one an eerie feeling; that was for sure. Black Eden, the new name, could not erase the horrific past of the place.

Nothing could.

Black Eden. That house was no paradise, not by a long shot.

Lord, have mercy.

Chapter Sixteen

The first two months at Black Eden were quiet and peaceful. Quite a few members of the church stopped by the mansion every-now-and-then to check on their new pastors, to see if they needed anything, and to see if they were comfortable in their new home. The members would stay for a few minutes then go on back into town.

But they were coming, and that made their pastors proud and grateful.

"Oh, these are some wonderful people," Ben never tired of saying.

Forrest had heard that statement more times than he cared to remember. His father was still trying to convince him that they had done the right thing by accepting the assignment and by moving into the mansion.

Because of his uneasy feelings, Forrest wanted to tell his father that he was wasting his breath trying to convince him that they had done the right thing. But he would give it more time. He didn't want to be too hasty as his father had already admonished him not to be.

He was in a *wait-and-see* mode. He wanted to be fair and not jump to conclusions too soon.

Yes, he had to admit that everything seemed wonderful. What could be more perfect than pastoring the biggest church in town, making more money than they had ever made in their whole lives, living in a mansion, and driving a spanking brand-new car?

What could be more perfect?

At the moment, he could not think of one thing.

I need to relax and enjoy, Forrest told himself.

And he tried. He, too, enjoyed all of the praise from, and the camaraderie he and his father had with, the members of the church. He, too, enjoyed the members when they came to visit. And, yes, he, too, was beginning to feel comfortable not only with the members and the church, but with their new environment, also.

They were beginning to feel as if this was where they belonged

Yes, the first two months were so peaceful, and so nice. Pastors Thomas and Thomas had settled into their new home, and were looking forward to a wonderful future as the new ministers of First St. Marks Baptist Church.

They had even had a few converts at the church, and had had one successful baptismal service.

They were on their way.

Their new church members had shown them that they would provide for them in a way neither of them had ever imagined. They were living like kings, and they were thoroughly enjoying the new lifestyle that had been granted them.

Forrest told himself that everything was on the up-and-up, and that he might have been wrong, that his mother might have been wrong, and that his father might have been right about the church.

He was ready to concede, and apologize to his father for doubting his wisdom.

Then the third month rolled around, and things changed—drastically.

Chapter Seventeen

Deacon Davis, a few of the other deacons, and Clarence Clark, the chairman of the trustee board, came by the mansion twice the first week of the third month to discuss what they said was church business with their new head minister.

For some reason, Forrest could not understand, he was shut out of those meetings.

"Just for the pastor's ears only," Deacon Davis said with a snide grin (that Forrest had grown to hate with a fervor) on his face when Forrest had asked why he could not attend the meetings.

If the meetings were about church business then why not?

"After all, I am the Assistant Pastor," Forrest argued.

"Yes, you are the *assistant,* and these meetings are not for the ears of the assistant pastor, just the senior pastor." Davis said, and everyone knew what Deacon Gaston Davis said pertaining to First St. Marks—and the whole town, for that matter, since he was the mayor—was law.

The two ministers had only been in town for a short while, but they, like everyone else in Clarksville, knew that Deacon Gaston Davis almost single-handedly ran the town and everything in it.

From what Forrest had already seen and heard, Davis even had the police force beckoning to his every command—right or wrong.

The secret meetings at the mansion soon escalated to three times a week: Monday, Thursday, and Friday.

Forrest wondered why these men were having so many covert meetings with his father. Ben had been pastoring for too many years to count. He knew what he was doing when it came to pastoring a church. He did not need guidance from anyone. He was capable of running First St. Marks the way a church should be run, unless there was something out of the ordinary going on at First St. Marks.

Forrest thought of his mother and the old woman. His mother simply had speculations about First St. Marks since she had no interactions with the church or any of its members. She was just listening to what others had to say and the newspaper articles that she had read. All of which could have been fabrications—even the newspaper articles since some reporters have been known to not thoroughly check out potential stories before reporting them.

But the woman, Mother McDonald, why would she spread untruths about the church she attended? The church she had been attending for years? Were her comments simply based on her feelings, her dreams?

Did she expect other people to base their relationship with the church on her dreams?

But he had heard of people who received messages from God in their dreams.

It was all too confusing.

But Forrest did know that after the meetings with Deacon Davis and his entourage, his father always looked tired, drained, and more and more withdrawn—as if something was really weighing on his mind. Whenever he asked his father what was wrong, Ben refused to discuss it with him.

"I'm just tired, Son," he would say. Then he would disappear into his room.

Even Ben's Sunday morning sermons began to suffer, and Forrest attributed that fact to whatever it was that was troubling him. Whatever those secret meetings were about was the problem.

He just knew it.

It was getting bad, and Forrest did not know what to do about it. He was concerned about his father's health, or more to the point, about his sanity.

His whole personality seemed to be changing. He did not seem like his upbeat, knowledgeable, God-centered self anymore. He did not seem like the father Forrest had known, loved, and wanted to emulate all of his life.

As much as Forrest did not want to believe it, his father's strange behavior and altered personality had begun shortly after the meetings with Deacon Davis and other officials of the church began.

Of course, Forrest had been curious. During the last few meetings at the house, he was compelled to listen outside the closed, and locked doors of the library. He was determined to find out as much as he could about what was happening to his father and why. The meetings had begun to get more heated each night—angry voices rising, and then quieting down again.

If one of the men had come to the door to check to see if he were listening to their conversations, Forrest had made up his mind that he would have welcomed being caught. Then he would just confront them outright. His father's health was more important than anything they could do to him.

He would not have minded being berated for standing up for his father, since the older man seemed to not be able to stand up for himself. Forrest thought it was his duty.

Forrest had not heard all of the conversations the nights he had been listening, but he heard enough to know that his father was being threatened.

"You'll do it or else, Ben!" That was the unmistakable voice of Deacon Davis. The man did not even have respect enough to address his new minister as Reverend or Pastor. After all, Ben was his pastor and should have been treated as such.

"I refuse to compromise my principles," he heard Ben's weak reply.

"Damn your principles. This is business," Davis again.

It was all Forrest could do to not pound on the door and demand that these disrespectful men stop their attack upon his father, their pastor. He wanted to kick all of them out of the house and tell them to never come back.

But he could not do that, because the house really belonged to them—well, to the church anyway. But he and his father were living in the house because of these very men: the powers-that-be at First St. Marks.

Yes, it was their house. He and his father were only guests in this stately mansion.

Forrest cringed when he recalled other parts of those heated conversations: "Why do you think you are here in this beautiful house?" the voice of one of the other men. *Deacon Miles,* Forrest thought.

". . . the huge increase in your salary." another voice that Forrest did not recognize.

On the last night that he listened outside the library, the conversation coming from the other side of the door was so soft, Forrest could barely hear a thing. Becoming frustrated, he finally gave up and went to bed.

He did not know how long those men stayed at the house that last night, how long they had tortured his father, and how long his father was going to allow them to treat him that way before he put a stop to it—even if it meant giving up the church of his dreams.

Forrest had to make Ben understand that what they had just obtained was not worth giving up their freedom, Ben's freedom to pastor the way he had groomed himself to do for the many years he had been pastoring. He was a learned man of the Bible. He had pastored two other churches before coming to First St. Marks. He had left those other churches of his own accord, and the members had been sorry to see him go. He was a good minister, a beloved pastor—until now—it appeared.

Chapter Eighteen

The next morning, when his father came down to breakfast, he looked as if the devil himself had been chasing him. Indeed, he probably had been in the form of the deacons and the chairman of the trustee board of the First St. Marks Missionary Baptist Church.

Forrest wanted to tell his father that he had heard the men threatening him, but he did not want to embarrass him or let him know that he had been listening to parts of their conversation.

But could he, in good conscience, just stand by and let whatever was going on continue, when he knew his father was being harassed? Even threatened?

Why? What were those meetings all about, anyway? What was so important that Davis and his bullying entourage thought it necessary to threaten his father?

"You'll do it or else, Ben."

That was surely a threat coming from the mouth of none other than the mighty Deacon Gaston Davis himself.

Forrest had to find out what was going on. He had to protect his father. But he had to first find out from what he had to protect him.

"Be careful what you pray for, because you might get it," Forrest whispered as he sat down to breakfast at the other end of the long table.

As usual, Mrs. Barber had outdone herself. The table was laden with a breakfast fit for the kings they had begun to feel like nowadays at the mansion. One thing he could truly say about First St. Marks was they knew how to stroke their prey. And that was what he was beginning to think he and his father were: prey.

"Good morning, Son," his father said.

"Morning, Dad."

Forrest watched as Ben picked at his food, finally eating a few pieces of the home-fried potatoes. He laid his fork down beside his plate, picked up his coffee cup, and drank a swallow. Over the next thirty minutes, he ate a few bites of the scrambled eggs, the bacon, the ham, the biscuits, and a little more of the home-fried potatoes.

Lord, please free my father of whatever has him so stressed he can't even eat, Forrest prayed silently. He ate. Mrs. Barber's efforts did not go to waste.

Forrest felt sorry for his father. The man was so disturbed, he couldn't even enjoy the foods he normally loved. Forrest wanted to help him. He wanted to reach out to him, comfort him as best he could, but he did not want to pry too much into what had occurred the nights before or his father might suspect that he had been eavesdropping.

Ben did not need any unnecessary distractions.

"Are you okay, Dad?" Forrest asked.

"Sure. Sure, Son. Just a little tired," Ben replied.

"Not hungry?"

"Got a lot on my mind."

I'll bet you do, Forrest thought. "Anything I can do to help?"

"I don't think so, Son. I'll be all right." Ben rose and laid his napkin gently over the uneaten food on his plate.

He turned to walk away then turned back and looked at his son for a moment as if he were about to speak, thought better of it, and turned again to leave.

Forrest leapt to his feet. "Talk to me, Dad. Talk to me! Tell me what's going on. What has you so upset you can't even eat! Talk to me!"

Ben stopped for a brief moment, his back still to his son, and then walked on out of the room.

Forrest watched his father leave the room, his gait slow and deliberate. He had almost confided in him. Forrest could see it in the older man's eyes: the burden, the toll this was taking on him. He wanted to share his burden, but he was afraid. Forrest could see the fear emanating from his father's face.

What was making him so fearful?

How could Forrest help him when he would not open up to him, his own son?

During the last couple of weeks, his father seemed to have aged at least ten years.

Forrest had to help him or he wasn't sure what was going to happen to the older man. He was deteriorating right before his eyes. How could a son watch this happening to his father and do nothing?

Forrest thought of the old woman and her prediction about the house. Could there really be something to what she said? Should they have listened to her and taken the parsonage beside the church instead?

Was the house really cursed?

Forrest raised his eyes toward the heavens. "Father, please show me what to do," he implored. He fell to his knees beside the chair in which he had sat, his eyes still imploring the heavens. "I'm losing my father, Lord. Help us! Help us, Lord!"

There was one thing Forrest knew without a doubt: prayer still worked.

Chapter Nineteen

It was Saturday morning of the third week of the third month that The Reverends Thomas and Thomas had been assigned the new ministers at the First St. Marks Baptist Church.

An impromptu meeting with Deacon Davis, his special group of Deacons and Clarence Clark was in progress in one of the meeting rooms at the church. Deacon Davis stood before the small group.

"It's not working," said Deacon Miles.

"No, it's not working exactly the way we planned," Davis said.

"He's real stubborn," Clark said.

Davis chuckled. "He has morals, principles."

The others smiled and chuckled, sharing the moment of levity.

"That's too bad," said Deacon Henry Sparks.

"Well, what are we going to do?" Clark asked.

"Break him down," Davis said matter-of-factly.

"He might not be that easily broken," said Deacon Sparks.

Davis chuckled. "Anyone can be broken. It might take a little longer than we anticipated."

"He wants all of the perks, but he doesn't want to work for them." This was from Deacon Miles.

"Oh, yes, he loves the perks," Davis again.

"I thought you said you checked him out before inviting him, Davis."

"I did," said Davis.

"I think we're wasting time. We either whip him into shape, or we don't," said Deacon Miles.

Clark sighed. "We *are* wasting time. Precious time. I think this meeting is a waste of time. There are a lot of things I could be doing on a Saturday morning."

"Just have a little patience, gentlemen. Give it time. It will happen." Davis assured the other men.

"Maybe we made a mistake," said Deacon Miles.

Davis smiled. "I don't think so, Deacon Miles. He's a single man, and just ripe for the pickings. We'll just go to Plan **B**."

The other men looked at Davis. Some smiled; some chuckled.

Davis guffawed. "Plan B, gentlemen."

"This should be fun," Clark said.

Chapter Twenty

"We can have the church on the tenth of December. We have to get busy," Sylvia said.

Forrest looked up at Sylvia, his face a mask of confusion. "What?"

"You're not even paying attention, Forrest. We need to plan our wedding. Where was your mind just now?"

"I'm sorry," Forrest said. "My father is having a rough time right now, and it's bothering me."

"What's going on?" Sylvia asked.

"It's just something to do with the church. I can't really talk about it."

"Why not? We're going to be married. We promised we wouldn't keep secrets from each other. Maybe I can help."

Forrest just looked at her, his silence telling all.

"So, you're telling me to mind my own business. Is that right?"

"It's not that, Sylvia. I promise you. It's just that I need to sort things out in my mind before I can talk with anyone— even you. I hope you understand." He smiled. "Let's plan our wedding, shall we?"

No, he wasn't sure what the problem was himself, and he knew involving other people, even his fiancée, in his uncertainties was not a good idea.

Sylvia looked at him skeptically.

Forrest took both to her hands in his. "Like I said, I can't talk about it just yet. The only business you and I need to be involved in right now is planning our wedding. Let's get to it, shall we?"

She smiled. "I'll buy that for right now."

"Thank you," he said.

"As I told you on the phone earlier today, the date for our wedding is the tenth of December." She kissed him on the lips.

"That sounds good to me," he said.

"I have already engaged ten of my friends for my bridesmaids."

"Ten bridesmaids? That's pretty big, don't you think?" Forrest could not believe what he had just heard.

She chuckled. "Yes, ten, and you are going to have to choose ten of your friends to be in your party."

"I've got to find ten guys who will want to stand up with me?"

"They might not want to, because they might be selfish enough to want you to stay single like they are, so you can spread your wild oats."

"I'm saving my wild oats." He gave her a quick smack on the lips. "And I do have a few married friends, also, you know."

She smiled at him. "Married or unmarried, they will do it, because they are your friends."

"Yes, they will. But ten?"

She laughed. "Ten."

"Our wedding party might fill up the church. Where are we going to put our guests?"

"Oh, stop it. "I plan to get married only once, so indulge me. I want my special day to be just that, special. A day I shall always remember, a day I can look back on and smile at our fiftieth anniversary."

"Fifty years. Do you think we're going to make it?"

She punched him gently on the shoulder. "We'd better."

"I think we can do that."

"I know we can. Oh, yes, and, of course, Melvetta, being my best friend, is going to be my maid of honor. And you are going to have to choose a best man."

"Whatever makes you happy."

"I'm happy just knowing that you love me, and that we shall be married soon."

"Soon," he said, and kissed her one more time.

⁂

There had been a toss-up as to who would marry them: Sylvia's pastor, the Rite Reverend Simpson, at Greater Rock, or Ben.

Since they were marrying at Sylvia's church, they decided to compromise and allow Ben to marry them.

Forrest hoped he would be up to the task.

⁂

Everything was in motion. It was going to be a beautiful wedding. Sylvia and her mother had decided on the right caterers—after stuffing themselves with samples of so many different foods they could not count them. The flowers had been ordered. Sylvia had chosen the floral arrangements she wanted and told the florist the order in which she wanted them placed at the church. He had promised her he would have her wedding decorations exactly the way she wanted them. The guest list had been composed, and invitations were ready to be mailed. Sylvia's maid of honor and her bridesmaids were ready and eager to share this special day with her and her groom-to-be; Forrest's best man and groomsmen were ready.

Then it happened.

Chapter Twenty-One

The choir was singing its last song: the song just before the sermon. Church had been in progress for approximately forty-five minutes.

The woman walked, no, she strutted, down the center aisle, her hips swaying in time to the music, her eyes fastened on something, or someone, on the dais. She wore a red dress, red shoes, a red pillbox hat, and carried a small red handbag that dangled from a single finger on her right hand—also keeping time with the music.

The dress fit her body snugly. But what a body it was. Even the sack dresses from the fifties could not have concealed a body like hers. The dress hung about midway her thighs and had a little flare at the hemline. The top came up around her neck. However, the pleated V-neckline did not do much to conceal the ample breasts that threatened to spill over any minute. Her jet-black hair that hung halfway down her back framed a face that would have put Cleopatra to shame. Her complexion was somewhere between olive and walnut. Her eyes were light brown. Her lips were full and rich and were painted cherry red just like her dress and other accessories.

The Reverends Thomas, father and son, saw her about the same time. Both of their mouths fell open, their eyes widened, and Forrest heard his father, who sat beside him, of course, begin to wheeze. He had not had an asthma attack in months. Now, all of a sudden . . .

The woman strolled all the way down the center aisle to the front pew, all eyes following her progress. She sat at the end of the seat—just off the center aisle and just to the left of the pulpit.

When she sat and crossed her legs, her skirt rose another three inches or so. Then she began to swing her left leg—that was crossed over her right—to the beat of the music, of course. The song ended, but the leg kept on swinging as if propelled by some secret switch that refused to turn it off.

The choir sat, and Ben stepped up to the pulpit. His eyes went directly to the woman-in-red, sitting on the front seat, with that leg that just kept on swinging, with her eyes focused right on him. He had told himself he was not going to look at her, and he had tried, but . . . It was as if his eyes had been drawn to her by a magnet. He couldn't help himself. It was as if he had no control over what his body was doing. His insides were lurching, and he thought if they did not stop, they would surely protrude right through his skin for all to see.

His eyes fell to that swinging leg. Then he remembered that hypnotists used some kind of swinging magnet to hypnotize their subjects? He jerked his eyes away from the woman's leg. They went to her face where a big smile played on her lips, her eyes still on him. He felt a bit dizzy, as if he might faint any minute. But he could not do that, now could he?

He had to preach.

Ben forced himself to look away—from the woman, from that smile, from those captivating eyes, from that swinging leg.

He cleared his throat, and opened his Bible. "Please turn with me to James, Chapter one, verses twelve through fifteen," he said to his congregation.

The Lord has certainly given me the right text for this Sunday morning, he thought.

Dr. Mildred Dumàs

"And the text reads," Ben continued. "'Blessed is the man that endureth temptation: for when he is tried, he shall receive the crown of life, which the Lord hath promised to them that love him.'" "Keep up with me now." He read on. "'But every man is tempted, when he is drawn away of his own lust, and enticed. Then when lust hath conceived, it bringeth forth sin; and sin, when it is finished, bringeth forth death.'"

He looked out over his congregation—the congregation he had been wanting for so many years, the congregation he had finally gotten, the congregation he wanted to keep. But if he were going to keep this new blessing that had been given him, he had to get himself together.

He had to get the distraction sitting on the front seat, in the blood red dress, out of his mind so he could do what he had been hired to do.

How had he chosen such an appropriate sermon for today? He was surely preaching to himself, because that woman was certainly getting under his skin.

Was God trying to tell him something?

"Death," he said. "Death, brothers and sisters. Death! Would a man lay down his life for his brother? Yes, definitely so. But for something as fleeting and temporal as lusting after the flesh? No! No, my brothers and sisters. No! Don't deceive yourselves. Be careful that you do not become transgressors of the law—God's law."

Ben preached on. The amens and hallelujahs were coming in on time. He was doing a good job.

Until his eyes wandered back to the front pew just a little to his right. The woman was still smiling at him. That same enticing smile, and as much as he did not want to admit it, that smile was doing its job.

It was definitely enticing him.

Had he heard a word he had just said to his congregation? Did he, their pastor, have the willpower to resist? Was he actually lusting after this strange woman? Was he? Could he resist the carnal feelings that were pushing through his mind?

Yes! Yes, he could. He had to do so, or he was doomed, and he knew it. He turned his eyes away from the woman, from that smile, from that swinging leg.

He had to get his mind back on his sermon.

Why had she come? Why was she smiling at him?

He was preaching his sermon, so why shouldn't she be looking at him? And if she were enjoying the sermon, why wouldn't she be smiling? It was all so innocent. She was young; looked to be in her mid-thirties perhaps. Maybe this was a new experience for her.

He pepped it up a bit bringing a few of the saints to their feet egging him on, and he did not disappoint them. He was back on track. He pushed on to a riveting ending. "Resist the devil, saints! Resist the temptation of whatever your particular vice might be. Resist, and the victory shall be yours!"

Ben closed his Bible, turned and took the few steps to his seat directly in back of the pulpit. He sat. Sweat poured down his face. He swatted it with his handkerchief. His insides were churning. Good, Lord, what was happening to him? Was he going to pass out right there on the podium?

Forrest looked at his father concernedly for a moment then got to his feet and went to the pulpit. The choir had already begun singing the song for opening the doors of the church. He did not want that choir director's eyes boring into him nor the pianist pounding on those ivories trying to get his attention.

"The doors of the church are open," he said.

The deacons rose and stood shoulder to shoulder on the floor in front of the podium. Several of them picked up chairs from the far side of the church, on their way up, and lined the chairs up on the floor in front of them—a deacon standing directly behind each chair, waiting for potential converts to come to Jesus.

"Is there one, today?" Forrest went on. "Is there one? Come, give your life to Jesus! He's waiting for you." He raised his arms in a welcoming gesture.

"Come. You don't have much time. He's waiting to receive you into the fold. Come. Don't waste another moment. Come!"

The woman on the front row, in the red dress, rose.

Forrest swallowed hard then forced a smile as the red clad woman strode over to one of the waiting chairs. He smiled at the woman. "Come on, Sister, give yourself to Jesus! Thank you, Lord! Is there another?"

The woman smiled at Forrest, and then at the deacon standing behind the chair she chose.

She sat and crossed her legs, eliciting a few grunts and groans from some of the female parishioners—especially from the Mothers' Bench.

There were no others.

One of the sisters from the Deaconess' Bench came forward with a pen, a tablet, and a lap cover in hand. She bent down and slapped the lap cover over the new convert's knees. The new convert looked up at the other woman, and then started to remove the cloth from her knees, until she saw the *I dare you look* the deaconess was giving her. She uncrossed her legs and sat like she guessed a proper lady should in church—knees covered and all.

The deaconess sat down beside the new convert, in one of the vacant chairs, and they conversed for a few moments.

When the choir finished singing, the deaconess rose, and looked toward the pulpit. "Pastor Benjamin, Pastor Forrest, associate ministers, and members of First St. Marks, we have with us today . . ." She read from her pad . . . "Ms. Conswella Cooper who is coming to us as a candidate for baptism."

"Hallelujah! Praise the Lord!" Forrest said.

Ben wiped frenziedly at the perspiration that was pouring down his face. "Praise Him! Praise Him!"

"Praise the Lord," chorused some of the deacons.

"Help us, Jesus," Mother McDonald said. She had seen the woman sashaying down the aisle just before the preacher got up to preach. She had seen the woman's eyes glued to the face of the preacher. She knew the woman was trouble. Big trouble was about to happen at First St. Marks. She sensed it. She could feel it in her spirit.

First St. Marks had some serious praying to do. They had been through so much already, and now this she-devil—that's what the woman was: the devil in the form of a woman—had joined them. Why? That's what she wanted to know. Why had this wayward creature come to First St. Marks?

But even as she asked herself that question, she knew.

"Oh, Lord," said one of the other ladies from the Mothers' Bench.

"Jesus!" said another.

"Lord, have mercy," came another exclamation from somewhere in the sanctuary.

Ben came down from the podium with his microphone. One of the deacons removed a microphone from a stand on the podium and gave it to the new convert who daintily removed the lap cover from her lap, stood, and laid it on her chair.

Ben took the hand of the new convert. "Welcome to First St. Marks, Ms. Cooper."

She held her microphone to her red lips and said in a soft, sultry voice, "Thank you, Pastor."

"Be assured that you have made the right decision this day, that giving yourself to Jesus is the best decision you have ever made in your life," Ben continued. He released her hand. "Tell me, Ms. Cooper, what are the reasons you feel this church is where God desires you to be?"

She smiled broadly, and looked him straight in the eyes. "Well, this church is close to my apartment. I was just driving down the street this morning, looking for a place to stop and worship, and the Lord just seemed to have guided me here."

Ben smiled broadly. "We're glad He did, Ms. Cooper."

There were a few *amens* from the congregation—mostly male voices—and the deacons.

Ben continued. "Tell me, Ms. Cooper, do you believe that Jesus died on the cross for your sins, and that on the third day, He rose from the dead?"

"Oh, yes I do, Pastor. I certainly do."

"And do you, Ms. Cooper, as a member of First St. Marks, agree to abide by the rules and regulations of this church?"

"I do," the new convert said, that captivating smile still on her face.

≈◍◕◍≈

"God be with you 'til we meet again," the congregation sang.

One of the associate ministers stood at the podium. He raised his right hand in the air. "Let us all sing . . ."

The pianist hit a cord, and they all sang, "Aaaaaaaaaaaaamen."

Pastor Benjamin Thomas, the Assistant Pastor, Forrest Thomas, and the associate ministers hurried down the aisle to the front of the church. The congregation filed out behind them.

As they stood, shaking hands and wishing the parishioners farewell, Ben spotted Mother McDonald coming toward them.

"Brace yourself. Here she comes," he whispered to his son.

"Who?" Forrest asked. He turned and saw Mother McDonald approaching.

Mother McDonald did not stop to shake their hands. She simply looked at them, and her eyes were blazing. "Watch out. The devil is on your track." She hurried on past them.

Then she was there in front of them: the woman in the red dress. Her eyes came to rest on Ben first. She held out her hand. He took it.

"Your sermon was wonderful, Pastor," she said in that same soft sultry voice. "It really got to me. I started thinking about that thing you said about sin bringing forth death, and I knew I did not want to die . . . yet." She smiled up at him, her eyes boring into his. "So, I thought I had better give myself to Jesus."

Ben smiled. "God bless you, my child." She was holding his hand a bit too long for just a handshake. He tried to pull his hand away; she held on to it.

"I do believe this is where God wants me to be," she said, her eyes glued to his face.

He tried again to pull his hand away and succeeded this time. It stood limply in the air for a moment; then he let it drop to his side. "Again, welcome, Sister Cooper. We're glad to have you," he managed to say.

Her eyes finally moved from his face. She turned her attention to Forrest, and offered her hand. He took it, and they shook.

"When you said, 'Give yourself to Jesus. You don't have much time,' I knew I just had to get up then and there and join the church. Your voice was so commanding, so masterful. I couldn't have sat there another minute if I had tried." She looked from one to the other of the two men standing before her. "Thank you, both of you, my new pastors."

She released Forrest's hand, turned and walked out the front door.

Both men's eyes followed her exit.

Chapter Twenty-Two

"Son, what did I tell you? They love us here." Ben sat at the head of the long dining table; Forrest sat at the other end. Ben loved this table. The hugeness of it made him feel big and important.

They should have a small dinner party soon. Not in the great room upstairs, but right here in this elegant room. The table would probably hold at least twenty-five to thirty people. They could open the doors and let it spill out onto the lanai. He could invite his old friends from Greater Rock. Let them see how he was doing. How he had moved up. Way up. This place represented his new-found worth, his new-found prestige, the appearance of wealth— even if that wealth was not really his. He loved this house. He loved everything in and about it.

He smiled.

Then his smile faded. Would that be bragging? *Of course not,* he thought, after a brief moment of serious deliberation. He was just so proud, and he wanted to share all of this with his friends.

Well, he would think about it, broach it to his son.

"I don't know, Dad. I'm having a few doubts," Forrest's voice cut into his thoughts.

Ben looked blankly at his son. "What? What did you say?"

"I said I'm having a few doubts about this whole thing."

"I just don't understand why you're such a doubting Thomas, Son.

"And I can't explain it to you, Dad. It's just an uneasy feeling."

"Well, I wish you could get rid of that uneasy feeling so you could start enjoying life."

They were finishing up their Sunday afternoon dinner of Cornish hens with wild rice stuffing, sautéed green beans, tossed green salad, whole wheat rolls and butter and fresh-squeezed lemonade. Warm peach cobbler was waiting in the kitchen for dessert.

Mrs. Barber had outdone herself again. One thing was for sure: these two preachers were more than satisfied with their cook slash housekeeper.

"Why? You don't believe all that hocus-pocus stuff that woman is talking, do you?"

"I don't know, Dad. There are bad and good in all walks of life, and remember what Brother Sheppard said."

"That might have been just a coincidence."

"I don't see how. Telling them to give up their vacation? Mother McDonald must have had a good reason. As it turned out, she did. Think about it, Dad. She saved those people's lives."

"That might have been just a good guess, Son. I think Mother McDonald is old and senile. That's what I really think."

"She says she sees things in her dreams. Some people do have that gift."

"Or curse."

"Oh, come on, Dad!"

"What do you want me to say, Son? We are being blessed, and I think we should be thankful, not skeptical. Why can't you just enjoy what the good Lord is doing for us?"

"I'm not so sure the Lord is behind all this, Dad."

"Let's just take it one day at a time. What do you say?"

"Sure, Dad." But Forrest wasn't so sure. He wasn't sure of anything anymore.

Mrs. Barber entered the room. "Excuse me."

They turned to her.

"Yes, Mrs. Barber?" Ben said.

"Uh, there's a young lady here to see you." Mrs. Barber looked uncomfortably from one to the other of the two men.

"Forrest or me?" Ben asked.

"Both of you," she said with a questioning look on her face.

"Who is it?" Ben asked.

"She said she preferred to surprise you."

Forrest chuckled. "Show her in."

"Yes, sir." Mrs. Barber turned and left the room.

"Who could it be?" Ben asked.

"Beats me," Forrest said. "We'll see in a minute." He continued to eat his dinner.

Ben sat waiting, his eyes glued to the doorway.

In a few moments, Mrs. Barber showed Conswella Cooper into the room.

"Sister Cooper," Ben said rising and extending his hand.

Forrest stood.

Conswella walked toward Ben, a big smile on her face. She was still dressed in that red dress.

She took Ben's outstretched hand. "My new pastor," she said, shaking his hand.

"Sister Cooper," Ben said again.

"Sister Cooper . . . Oh, I like that, Pastor, everybody calling everybody sister and brother. I'm already enjoying being a member of First St. Marks," Conswella said, the smile never leaving her face. She let her hand linger in Ben's for a few moments longer then released it, and turned to Forrest. "And my other new pastor," she said taking Forrest's extended hand, pumping it slowly.

"Sister Cooper," Forrest said. "To what do we owe this Sunday afternoon visit?"

Conswella chuckled. "Well . . . "

Ben pulled out a chair from the table. "Please, have a seat, Sister Cooper."

"Thank you," she said. She slid into the chair, and crossed her legs.

The men sat back down at the table.

"I'm fairly new in town," Conswella continued. "As I said at the church, I've been looking for a church home for a few weeks now. I heard about First St. Marks, and about you, the new ministers." Her eyes slid from one of the men to the other. "Talk is all over town, you know."

"Is that right?" Forrest asked.

"Yes, it is, Pastor Forrest. Can you imagine my surprise when I looked up and saw that tall steeple and the name, First St. Marks Baptist Church, while driving around looking for a church this morning? I could not believe my eyes, and I knew it must have been fate that led me in that direction."

"Humph! That is strange, Sister Cooper. It really is," Forrest said, a skeptical look on his face.

She chuckled. "That's right. How odd was that?"

"Pretty odd, I must admit," Forrest said.

"But that is exactly what happened, and I thought it had to be an omen, that First St Marks was the place I should be. I could feel the love when I walked through the door, and that confirmed my feelings. Your church is where I belong."

"Again, Sister Cooper, we're glad to have you with us," Ben said.

"Thank you, Pastor," she said. "I've also heard so much about your house. Black Eden I believe they call it?" It was more a question than a statement.

"Yes. I gave it that name," Ben said smiling broadly.

"Oh, how ingenious! And it's so befitting. From what I've heard and seen so far, your new home is absolutely breathtaking."

"Thank you," Ben said.

"I wasn't around for your welcoming banquet, and I had absolutely nothing on my agenda this afternoon, so I thought I would come out and see if you would give me a little tour."

"Well, Sister Cooper we—" Forrest began.

"We'd be happy to show you around, Sister Cooper. We're glad you came," Ben said.

"I'm so sorry I interrupted your dinner. Please forgive me. I was just so eager, and I thought a leisurely Sunday afternoon would be a perfect time."

"Yes, well . . ." Forrest made a defeated gesture, and left the sentence dangling.

"Oh, please forgive my manners," Ben said. "Have you eaten, Sister Cooper?"

"Well, I had a little something right after I left the church."

Ben waved a hand toward the table. "Feel free to join us. We could have our housekeeper bring you a plate. She's a great cook."

"No, I'm fine, thank you. Why don't I just wait in the living room, or parlor? Which do you call it? I noticed it off the hallway as Mrs. Barber showed me in to see you."

Ben chuckled. "Well, the fine ladies of the church say it's a parlor, so I guess that's what we'll call it, too."

"Looks like a living room to me," Forrest offered.

Conswella laughed. "Well, why don't I just go sit in the parlor slash living room while you finish your dinner? And, again, I'm so sorry for interrupting you." She rose.

"Oh, I was about finished," Ben said. He looked at Forrest. "How about you, Son?"

"Yes, I've finished, also. I guess we can have dessert later," Forrest offered.

Conswella smiled sweetly at them.

"Great idea," Ben said then turned back to Conswella. "We'll give you the tour then perhaps you would join us for dessert, Sister. Cooper. Mrs. Barber, our housekeeper is also our cook, and she makes the best peach cobbler in the world."

Conswella beamed at him. "Peach cobbler? Now that sounds wonderful. If you're sure it would be all right."

"We're sure. You're welcome to stay," Ben said.

"Thank you. I would love to."

Ben turned. "This way."

Conswella and Forrest followed Pastor Benjamin out of the room.

Chapter Twenty-Three

"That was absolutely delicious," Conswella said, patting her stomach. "And you are absolutely right, Pastor Benjamin. Mrs. Barber does make the best peach cobbler in the world, or the best I've ever tasted anyway."

Ben sat at the head of the dining room table, Conswella sat to his right, and Forrest sat at his usual spot at the other end. The tour was over and they were finishing up dessert.

"Yes, Mrs. Barber is a great cook," Ben said.

Conswella smiled at him. "She certainly is. I've tasted a lot of peach cobblers, and that was really the best I've ever had, and I'm a country girl."

"No," Ben said.

"Yes, I was born and reared in Mississippi."

"You don't talk like a country girl," Forrest said. *And you certainly don't act like one,* he thought.

She chuckled. "I cleaned up my country act when I moved to the Mid-West—St. Louis, Missouri to be exact.

"So, it's not true when people say that you can take a person out of the country, but you can't take the country out of the person?" Forrest asked.

Conswella laughed then cooed at him. "You be the judge."

"In your case, I guess not," Forrest said.

Ben smiled broadly at Conswella. "He's right. If you ever had any country in you, you certainly did a good job of leaving whatever you had in you behind, but now you're back in the country."

"Yes, I'm back to living the good country life again."

Forrest looked at his father. The man was actually gawking at the woman, grinning from ear-to-ear, and she was laying on the charm.

"Would you like some more peach cobbler, Sister Cooper?" Forrest asked. He had to try to divert his father's attention somehow. He could not believe what he was seeing. The two of them were acting like a couple of love-sick teenagers. What in the world was his father thinking? Was he actually falling for the woman's antics? A woman young enough to be his daughter. . .?

"No, thank you," Conswella said, her eyes glued to Ben's smiling face. "I've had enough of . . . the pie. I have to watch my figure."

Ben chuckled. "I don't think you have to worry too much about that, Sister Cooper."

The man is actually blushing, Forrest thought. "Dad?"

Ben looked blankly at his son. "Yes?"

"Would you like more pie?" Forrest asked.

"No. No, thank you. I've had enough."

"I guess I should be going." Conswella got up from the table. "Thanks for the tour and the dessert. You have a beautiful home. This is about the most gorgeous place I've ever seen in my life. You must enjoy staying here so much."

"Yes, we do," Ben said.

Conswella beamed at Ben then Forrest. "Oh, I'd give anything to live in a place like this. There are so many wonderful rooms. And the great room is absolutely spectacular. I'm sure your welcoming banquet was a grand affair and that you're going to have many more gatherings of that sort up there. And now that I'm a member of the church . . ." Her eyes fastened on Ben's smiling face. ". . . I do hope I'll be invited."

I'll just bet you do, Forrest thought.

"Of course, The next time we have a gathering, I'll make sure you get an invitation," Ben said.

"Oh, and the twin bay windows upstairs, with that lovely bench in between them, is precious. Perfect for relaxing with a good book," she cooed.

"Yes, I like that spot, too. It is perfect for relaxing," Ben agreed.

She smiled at him and offered him her hand. He took it, and they shook. "Thank you, Pastor. I shall look forward to your next gathering." She released his hand.

Forrest took her by the elbow. "I'll show you out, Sister Cooper."

Conswella smiled up at him. "Oh, I just can't get over my new identity: Sister Cooper. I think I'm going to like being a good Christian lady."

Forrest chuckled and tightened his grip on her elbow, moving her forward.

She smiled back over her shoulder and waved at Ben. "Goodbye, Pastor. I'll see you Wednesday night at Bible study."

Ben waved back at her. "See you then, Sister Cooper."

She stopped, pulled her arm free of Forrest's grasp, and turned back to Ben. "Oh, yes, Pastor, when am I going to be baptized?"

"The first Sunday in next month. Baptism is always on the first Sunday."

"I feel so honored." She cooed at him. "Bye."

Forrest took her elbow again and ushered her toward the exit.

"Feel free to come back anytime, Sister Cooper," Ben said to their retreating backs.

"Thank you. I just might take you up on that, Pastor," Conswella said over her shoulder, her voice dripping sweetness.

Ben looked after his son and the woman until they were out of sight.

That's some lady, he thought.

Chapter Twenty-Four

"What do you think of our new member?" Ben asked. He and Forrest sat on the front porch sipping iced tea. It was about an hour after their unexpected guest had left.

"I think the woman's coming on to you, Dad?"

"Me? Coming on to me? You would be more her type, and age, don't you think?"

"I'm not the pastor. You are. I'm just your lowly assistant. I think Sister Cooper is reaching for the top."

Ben laughed. "Don't be silly. But she's really something, isn't she?"

"Indeed, she is. Just showing up out here without so much as a phone call."

"Oh, that was all right. We encourage our members to drop by whenever they are in the area."

Forrest shook his head. "She wasn't in the area, remember? She didn't have anything on her calendar this afternoon, so she just decided to pay us a surprise visit." He chuckled. "I don't know, Dad. That was rather strange if you ask me."

"Don't be so skeptical of others, Son. She was free this afternoon, and she wanted to see the house. People have been talking about this place, the new name, us . . . so much that it's enough to stir anyone's curiosity."

"I know we're not supposed to judge others, Dad, but that woman made me just a little uncomfortable here at the house and at the church earlier. From the beginning, the way she slithered down that aisle at the church, all the way to the front row where she decided to sit in that short, revealing red dress."

Ben laughed. "Yes, that dress is something. But . . . slithered?"

Forrest chuckled. "Yes, the woman slithered. I don't know how else to describe that walk down that aisle, do you?"

"It was some walk, wasn't it?"

"It caused every head in the church to turn, even on the podium. I declare, Dad. It was as if time stood still for the few moments it took her to walk down that aisle. I know my head turned, and out of the corner of my eye, I could see your head turn on the right side of me, and the head of Minister Ford who was on the left of me. I could not see the heads of the other ministers who were sitting up there with us, but I have a feeling they turned as well."

Ben guffawed. "I guess that was a head-turning event, Son. Her presence at the church was rather distracting."

That red dress . . . he had never, before in his entire life, seen a red dress worn like that woman was wearing that red dress. The Missionary Societies of the two other churches he had pastored always wore red on the fifth Sunday, so he had seen a lot of red dresses, but he had to declare, that red dress that Sister Cooper was wearing—still—was about the most captivating red dress he has ever seen in his life.

There was just something special about that woman and her red dress.

Forrest chuckled. "I don't have to guess about it, dad. I know it was. I'd be willing to wager that that woman made just about every man in First St. Marks uncomfortable. And lucky us . . . we got a double dose since we were on the podium, right in the line of fire."

They both laughed.

"I suggest we get that woman and that red dress out of our minds and concentrate on your sermon today. It was a good one and right on time," Forrest said.

"Thank you, Son. I was preaching from my heart." He chuckled. "But let's give the lady a break. Yes, her actions were rather questionable, but now that she has turned her life over to the Lord, let's just wait and see, shall we?"

"That would be the Christian thing to do, wouldn't it?"

"Yes, it would. And you know, here at the house, in a more relaxed atmosphere, I felt quite comfortable around her."

"Sorry I can't say the same."

"Beautiful women are everywhere, Son. We see them all the time."

"I agree. But there's just something about that one." Forrest chuckled. "Now can we change the subject?"

Mrs. Barber came through the front door carrying a pitcher. "More tea, gentlemen?"

Ben held up his glass. "Yes, thank you, Mrs. Barber. It sure does hit the spot."

"No, thanks, Mrs. Barber, I think I've had enough." Forrest said.

Mrs. Barber re-filled Ben's glass, turned, and went back into the house.

The men soon tired of the front porch. They went into the house and watched television for a while; then the Reverends, father and son, went to bed.

Later, they both dreamed about their new convert, the lady in the red dress.

Chapter Twenty-Five

"Mom and I mailed the invitations today," Sylvia said.

Sylvia and her mother, Verlene, had worked for hours, addressing and then mailing the invitations to her and Forrest's impending wedding. Sylvia's best friend and Maid of Honor, Melvetta, had promised to help but had canceled at the last minute because of an emergency.

"I'll make it up to you somehow," Melvetta said when she called just as Sylvia and Verlene sat down to begin the long, arduous task.

Sylvia meant to hold her to that promise, because she and her mother had to work overtime to make up for the extra help that did not show.

Sylvia and Verlene were both tired. Verlene had lain down to take a much-needed nap. Sylvia thought about doing the same, but when Forrest called and asked her out to dinner, new found vigor assailed her. She loved this man; she loved being with him, and could not wait to become his wife.

Needless to say, the wedding had taken over her life now. It was her waking thought every morning and the last thing she thought about before falling asleep at night.

"I'd love to go out to dinner after a long day of laboring over those invitations," she replied.

"Good, I'll pick you up in a few," Forrest said.

They sat in small Soul Food Restaurant. Dinner was over, and they were waiting for their dessert.

"Thanks for dinner. It was a pleasant surprise," Sylvia said.

"Glad to be of service, my lady. I heard they had great food here and thought you might like it."

"And you were right. My turkey wings and dressing, smothered cabbage, and candied yams dinner was simply delicious. They should do well."

Jimmie's Soul Food was a new restaurant in town, and from the looks of the crowd inside and those waiting to be seated, it was an instant success.

"My fried catfish dinner was good, too," Forrest said.

"They have so many excellent choices," Sylvia offered.

"I hear they have two brothers from New Orleans in the kitchen, and from what I have heard, and what I tasted this evening, those brothers know how to throw down," Forrest said.

They chuckled.

"I have to agree." Sylvia said.

She smiled across the table at her fiancé. At that moment, Sylvia Madden knew, without a doubt, that she was the happiest, and the luckiest woman in the world.

As hard as Forrest tried to keep his mind on his fiancée, it kept flashing back to his dream of the night before that the woman in the red dress had invaded. She was all inside his head. The woman was messing with his mind. Who was she? What was she? From where had she come? Why had she come? And why was her coming upsetting him so much?

That was one reason he had wanted to see Sylvia tonight, to try to sort out the strange things that were going on in his head.

Then he thought about his father and how haggard and tired he had looked at breakfast that morning, as if he had tossed and turned all night, also. When he asked the older man what the matter was, he had mumbled something totally unintelligible.

Forrest decided to let it alone and chalked it up to his father's dread of meeting with the group from the church that evening.

He checked his watch. They would be there within the hour.

He had to get Sylvia home then hurry back to the mansion as fast as he could just in case his father needed him. Not that they would allow him inside the library where the meetings were always held, but at least he wanted his father to know that he was there in the house if he needed him.

"Forrest!" Sylvia looked at her husband-to-be. "Come back, Reverend Thomas," she teased.

"Huh? Oh, I'm sorry. What were you saying?"

"I was asking if you had engaged your tuxedo yet. You said you were going to do it the other day."

"Not yet, but I'll get to it. I promise. I have plenty of time."

"How about your best man and your groomsmen; are they ready?"

"We'll all do it at the same time. Don't worry."

"There might be a lot of activities going on around that time, and you might have to end up buying instead of renting."

"I've got it under control. Believe me."

She chuckled. "All right, you're on your own. The girls and I are going to look for dresses Monday. We're meeting downtown after work."

"Uh huh." He was getting married. He was actually sitting here planning his wedding. He was marrying the woman he loved.

So why did his mind keep wandering? Why was his head still full of Miss? Mrs.? Ms.? He was going to make it his business to find out who Conswella Cooper really was. Why couldn't he get her and that red dress off his mind? Why couldn't he keep his mind on his fiancée and his impending wedding?

He could not answer any of those questions.

Their dessert finally came. Forrest breathed a sigh of relief. Time was passing, and his father was alone at the mansion.

Chapter Twenty-Six

They'll be here in a few minutes, Ben thought. He had to prepare himself for the onslaught. That's what it was, plain and simple. What they wanted him to do was unconscionable. But they had ordered, yes ordered, not asked, but ordered him to do it. But how could he do what they were insisting and still hold his head up and proclaim to be a minister, a man of the cloth, God's servant? How could he explain his actions?

But it didn't seem to bother the others, so why should it bother him?

He thought about this long and hard and came to the conclusion that it bothered him, because he was an honest man. Honesty, pride, and dignity . . . they all had been engrained in him. They were the traits of a good man, a righteous man, and he was. He went even beyond the man. He was a minister, for God's sake. People looked up to him, told their children to respect him, to obey the words that spewed from his mouth when he stood at the pulpit.

How could he betray their trust? He could not, not in good conscience anyway. There was no acceptable explanation. It was exploitation plain and simple. They wanted him to help them exploit the people, the people of God, his new congregation, his new charges. Yes, he was in charge of those people. He was their new pastor, their leader. He was supposed to lead them in the right direction, help them when they faltered on their Christian journey, when they needed counseling, when they thought all hope was gone, when they . . .

If he followed the directives of those men, he would be in violation of his promises to God. He would need someone to counsel him, to get him back on the right track.

He could not do what they were demanding of him. He just could not do it.

How could he honestly face those people, some of them senior citizens, little old men and women who were living on fixed incomes? How could he face himself? Could he ever look in the mirror with a clear conscience again?

Deacon Davis and his pack of bloodhounds were banking on the congregation adhering to the pleas they wanted him to make from the pulpit. But it was just not right.

Then why was he pondering over his decision? Why couldn't he make the right one? Because he would be out of a job—his new job that he had coveted for so many years. Oh, how he had prayed for this parish. He had stayed on his knees night after night, year after year. He had begged and pleaded with the Lord to hear his prayers and grant him this blessing.

And now that he had all that he thought he needed to make his life's journey in the ministry complete, he was about to lose it.

"Be careful what you pray for," he had told many of his parishioners who had come to him with their problems.

Perhaps he should take his own advice.

But Davis had promised him the house. He had actually promised to sign the mansion over to him. It would be his, not the church's house anymore, but his. His. Things were getting better for him every day.

All he had to do was . . .

He wondered if this was really a blessing or a curse. Maybe his late wife had been right after all. Maybe his son's trepidations about all this was a warming sign.

From God?

And the old woman . . . He could not get her out of his mind. She had warned him about the house. But what did the house have to do with anything? What did it matter if he and his son stayed in the parsonage or this beautiful mansion that had everything they ever wanted—and a few that they didn't. The slave quarters out back, a harsh reminder of the despicable conditions in which some of his race had been forced to live. The hanging tree—all reminders of a past that he would rather forget. But, of course, he couldn't forget. No one in his or her right mind could. It was history, and this part of the history of Clarksville, Arkansas would remain as long as the Lizzie Cochran mansion stood. Sister Cochran had seen to that.

But when he became owner . . .

The good about the mansion overshadowed the bad. My, Lord, they even had a maid. What other ministers could say such a thing? The ones on television, of course, and maybe a few others had chauffeurs, chefs, maids, and butlers, but it was totally unheard of for ministers of his caliber. This was a first for him, and he loved every bit of it. Yes, he did.

Maybe too much.

This place is like a palace, and I feel like a king in it. I can't just walk away from all of this. At last I have arrived. Any other minister would give his soul to have what I have finally been granted, he thought.

"Thank you, Jesus," he said out loud, but not as forcefully as he had been extolling this phrase. His mind was in such turmoil.

Am I doing the right thing? he wondered. "Lord, help me!" he implored.

Then he thought of the woman in red. She had come to him in his dreams. What had that meant? Why had she come to him? Was she in trouble? Did she need his help? Did she possibly need counseling? Was the Lord directing him to help his new member with some pressing problem? But . . . Her visit to him, in his dream, did not seem to be of an innocent nature. It was more like . . .

No, he would not think of that young woman in that way. He was reading things into what was probably just an innocent cry for help. He would have to make himself available if the woman needed him. After all, he was her pastor. That was part of his job.

And in order to keep his present job . . .

They had given him one week. He had one week to think about his life—if he wanted to keep it as it was now, or if he wanted to go back to being a poor, begging beat-down preacher who was barely making it in a land of plenty.

It just wasn't fair. God's people should have all of their needs met plus some of their desires. Hadn't the Lord said, 'Ask and it shall be given? Seek and ye shall find?' Didn't He say he would pour out blessings that there would not be room enough to receive?

Well, his blessings were coming one right after the other, and he could not give them back. He just could not. That would be like saying, "I don't want your blessings, Lord. Give them to someone else."

He had had a brief taste of the luxurious life-style of the haves—even if what he had now was not yet in his name, even if someone else owned the titles to the house and the car. The house was still his in which to live; the car was his to drive. All of it was his as long as . . .

He would try again to make them see how wrong their requests, no, not requests, but orders, were. Maybe he could make them see reason.

If not . . . No, he would not think of what might happen if he did not do their bidding.

The house . . . Davis said it would be his soon. But could he rely on what Davis said? He had already shown him that he was not a good person, not the person he presented to the public or to his fellow church members.

He had thought the man was a saint—at first—he and the other men on his special committee. But Ben knew that sometimes looks could be deceiving, and in this case, they were extremely so.

If a person would lie . . .

Why could he not have seen it? Why had he been so blind?

Oh, he knew. He had been blinded by all the glamour, the gifts, and the promises.

The doorbell rang, bringing Ben out of his reverie. He looked fearfully in the direction from which the sound came.

Chapter Twenty-Seven

He was late. They were already there. He saw the cars even before he pulled into the circular driveway. The leader of this posse from the prestigious First St. Marks Baptist Church had even blocked the garage entrance. Well Forrest would just block his exit. He parked directly behind the white Rolls Royce. Maybe he would go on upstairs and go to bed, go to sleep.

He was not a light sleeper by any means, so when the great Mr. slash Mayor Gaston Davis finished harassing his father, he would have to wait a while before being able to leave his unauthorized parking space.

The man was a major liberty taker.

Some people . . .

Forrest went on into the house. He stopped momentarily outside the closed library door. He heard nothing. Either they were talking very softly or there was a long lull in their conversation. Or, maybe they were in the midst of silent prayer. After all this was a church group, a church meeting — supposedly anyway. Prayer would certainly be a good way to begin their meetings. Surely, they opened and closed their meetings with prayer. After all, they were the good, God-fearing leaders of the First St. Marks Baptist Church.

God only knew what was going on in that room.

They're all a bunch of hypocrites, Forrest thought. Prayer probably wouldn't do any of them a bit of good. They were all going straight to hell as far as he was concerned.

He had to have a long talk with his father. He would try to wait up for him. No, he had to wait up because of the white Rolls Royce, didn't he?

"The nerve," he mumbled to himself.

He went into the kitchen and made himself a cup of instant coffee. They had a pot of Mrs. Barber's freshly brewed coffee in that room. He had a good mind to walk right in there and get a cup. Well, he couldn't just walk right in, because they always had the door locked which made him look like an idiot.

He put cream and sugar in his instant coffee, and went into the family room to watch television.

"Next Sunday," Gaston Davis was saying.

Ben sat in the midst of Davis and his committee, made up of some of the Deacons and the head of the Trustee Board from First St. Marks. Ben had no allies at these meetings. He stood alone. All of the other men seemed to be on the same wavelength, a wavelength that was totally different from his.

There were a few of the Deacons from the church who were not asked to be members of this special committee. Ben assumed they were the decent ones who could not be bought, the ones Davis knew would not go along with his underhanded tactics to secure his position as mayor of the fine city of Clarksville for another term.

Ben made a mental note that he would have to speak with some of those deacons.

"Ben, are you listening?" Davis asked.

"I can't do it, Deacon Davis. I just can't. It's wrong. It's wrong," Ben protested.

"There are many things that are wrong with this world, Ben. It was wrong for us to use church funds to give you that new car, but we did," Davis said. "We could have let you continue to drive that old Cadillac you were driving when you came to us begging to be our new pastor, but we didn't. We bought you a spanking brand-new Mercedes Benz, because we want our pastor to look good."

And we didn't offer you the parsonage at the church; we set you up here in this exquisite place," Deacon Miles offered.

Deacon Sparks smiled and waved his arms about the magnificent room. "This stately mansion."

"That will soon be all yours," Davis chimed in.

"First St. Marks has a reputation to live up to, Ben. That's just how we operate," Clarence Clark, the chairman of the trustee board, said,

"Have you at least broached this to the congregation? Do they know?" Ben asked.

"That's beside the point," Davis said. "The fact is I need your help now. Turn about is fair play, don't you think?"

"I want my new congregation to trust me, to depend on me to look out for their best interest. I can't do that if I'm dictating inappropriately from the pulpit," Ben said.

"No disrespect, Pastor, but we've been going back and forth about this all week. You have to decide, once and for all, whether you want First St. Marks or not. I have to get up early in the morning. It's time to go," said Davis. He stood.

"You're on the clock, Ben," said Deacon Sparks. He rose.

Ben was beside himself with grief. He had to make them understand. "Listen! You have to listen. We can't scam our church members. We can't rob them. That's what we would be doing: stealing from God's people!"

"We've listened long enough, Ben. Now, you listen to the following questions, and think long and hard before you make your decision: Do you want to remain here as pastor of First St. Marks? Do you want this mansion? Do you want to keep your new Mercedes-Maybach Luxury Sedan? Or don't you? It's as simple as that," Davis said as he led the other men to the door.

Davis unlocked the door, and he and his followers filed out of the library.

Ben followed, his head bowed, his expression grave. How could he do what they wanted? How could he? He would be deceiving his flock, the people he had been entrusted to lead in a good Christian manner.

But if he did not do as these men ordered . . .

He did not want to think about that now. He could not lose his newfound lifestyle. He just got it, and was about to lose it in a matter of months? God would not play such a trick on him. He had served Him most of his life. He was a good man. It was about time something good came his way. And it had, and he wanted to keep it.

He had to keep it, especially the house, and, of course, his position as pastor of First St. Marks, but . . .

He walked with the other men to the front door without another word. There was nothing else to say, he assumed. They had made up their minds, and, they had told him what he had to do. He had argued as best he could. God knew he had. He had told them how ungodly he thought their demands were. How unchristian-like it would be to fleece God's people. How he was a good God-fearing man who could not, in good conscience, do what they were so heartlessly demanding.

All to no avail.

But Ben knew he was right. They knew he was right, but doing the right thing did not seem to matter to them just so they got what they wanted, and they did not care whom they hurt in the process.

The bottom line was: if he did not do as they wished, he was going to be relieved of all the good things that had just come his way, and those that were about to be realized. He would be right back where he started.

He had just been instated, and now he was being threatened with expulsion from the post he had craved for as long as he could remember. And the house, this fabulous bonus that came with the post—that was soon to be his. And the car . . . He was becoming so comfortable driving his new automobile.

He was living the life he had always wanted: the good life, a life without worry.

Ben's mind was full of what his life would be like if all that he had just received was snatched away from him. And he was worried about his reputation, his good, upstanding reputation. It had taken him years to build up that reputation, years of good Christian living, good honest living. Could he give it all up for what he had now? Was it too much of a sacrifice?

Maybe.

But other ministers were living like kings here in America— the land of the free, the land of opportunity. Why shouldn't he?

God wants his people to prosper, he thought. He had begun to prosper.

Maybe . . .

"Next Sunday," Deacon Davis said cutting into Ben's thoughts, as he and the other men went down the front steps.

Ben closed the door and walked back up into the house.

"Is everything all right, Dad?"

Ben whirled about to face his son. "I didn't hear you come in."

"I was waiting up until they left. Is everything okay?"

"Sure. Sure. I'm just a little tired. I'm going to turn in."

"What did Deacon Davis mean when he said next Sunday?'"

The doorbell rang. Ben jumped about, an agonized look on his face.

My God, he looks as if he's scared out of his wits, Forrest thought. "It's just Deacon Davis. I have him blocked in," he said.

"You blocked him in?" Ben asked.

The look of sheer terror that Forrest saw on his father's face told him that Ben was actually afraid of the man.

My God, this is serious, Forrest thought. "Sure did," he said. "He blocked the entrance to the garage."

"But—" Ben began.

"But nothing, Dad. He's too high and mighty for his own good."

The doorbell rang again. Forrest opened the door.

"I'm blocked in!" Deacon Davis' voice was loud and angry. He looked at Forrest with total disdain.

"You blocked the garage," Forrest said. He smiled at the irate man.

"Sorry," Deacon Davis muttered as he turned and walked to his car.

Forrest went out the door and closed it behind him. *Maybe he'll find another place to park next time, he thought.* Somebody needed to bring that man down to size.

In a few minutes, Forrest re-entered the house. Ben was standing at the window, peeking around the curtains. He turned to his son, a frightened look on his face, as if blocking the great Deacon in was a crime that could cost him his life.

"Couldn't you have found another place to park?" Ben asked.

"At my own house?" Forrest shot back. "Couldn't he have found another place to park? Out on the street perhaps? That man takes too many liberties."

"I'm going to bed," the older man said. He turned and walked off toward the stairs.

"What was that about next Sunday, Dad?"

"It was nothing, nothing." Ben continued on up the stairs.

Forrest watched his father until he was out of sight in the upstairs hallway. The older man looked so worn and weary, and frightened beyond belief.

What in the world are they doing to him? Forrest thought. Just what had Deacon Davis meant when he said next Sunday?

It sounded like a threat to him. What was going to happen next Sunday?

Forrest looked about at the opulence that surrounded him. This beautiful, stately, mansion and all of its status-invoking amenities and pleasures were beginning to take its toll on his father already. They had just gotten here, and to see so much of a change in his father was frightening. He just did not know what to think. He was at a loss.

"It's not worth it?" he said to himself.

His father was not usually a gullible man, but these people were changing him, getting to him in a way Forrest could not have ever imagined.

He had always been so proud of his father and his ideals, his moral stance on every situation in which he had been involved—in the past. But now . . . This was a first, an enigma. What were they going to do about it?

What could they do?

They could leave this place. Put as much distance between it and them as they possibly could. But could he persuade his father to do so?

He did not think so. It was as if his father had on blinders. All that mattered was the new ministerial appointment, the huge salary, the car, and this enormous house.

He was tired. He needed to rest, get some sleep. He would talk with his father in the morning.

Forrest went upstairs and walked down the long hallway toward his room.

"God help us," he whispered as he approached his father's closed bedroom door. He stopped momentarily and looked at the solid oak door. *I wonder what's going through his mind right now?* He thought. He shook his head, turned and walked on down the hallway to his own room.

"Help us, Jesus," he whispered. As he closed his bedroom door.

Chapter Twenty-Eight

Take me to the water to be baptized.

The choir and congregation of First St. Marks sang. It was the first Sunday, and the church was preparing for its newest convert to be baptized. Baptism was always scheduled right after Sunday morning *"praise and worship."*

Both Pastor Ben and Pastor Forrest were in the baptismal pool that was stationed just above, in back of, and in the center of the choir stand. They both wore white robes over white shirts and pants (old clothes they kept at the church just for this occasion). After the baptism, they would change back into their suits for the morning service.

Their candidate for baptism, First St. Marks' newest member, Sister Conswella Cooper, approached the pool. She was accompanied by Sis. Louise Murray, one of the deaconesses. Conswella also wore a white robe. On her head was a white shower cap, to protect her hair when she went down into the liquid grave. Her face was made up to perfection—as always. Her feet were bare. Her toenails were painted a bright red just like her lips.

She looked down at her pastors and smiled.

None but the righteous . . .

None but the righteous . . . The choir and congregation sang on.

Conswella stepped down into the water, her hands outstretched—reaching for her new pastors who stood at the bottom of the steps, each with a hand outstretched, waiting to guide their new convert to the middle of the pool for her emersion.

They each took a hand and did so.

They stood facing the sanctuary, the ministers, one on either side of Conswella. They locked arms—at the wrists—in back of Conswella to support her when they dipped her into the water.

Ben raised his right hand. "Sisters and Brothers . . ." The choir and the congregation stopped singing. ". . . coming to us today for baptism is Sister Conswella Cooper." He paused a moment then went on. "In obedience to the great head of the church, and upon the profession of your faith, Sister Cooper, we baptize you in the name of the Father, and of the Son, and of the Holy Ghost!" Ben put his right hand over Conswella's nose, and then he and Forrest dipped her backwards into the water.

Conswella came up out of the water with her hands in the air. "Hallelujah!" she shouted and began to shake her upper body. The wet robe clung snugly to her now. Her ample breasts, with nipples standing at attention, were outlined perfectly by the wet garment. They swayed from side to side, and seemed to be trying to poke holes right through the front of her baptismal attire.

"Oh, my God," Forrest said under his breath.

Ben was having a hard time trying to keep his eyes off the swaying breasts. Forrest began to propel Conswella toward the steps down which she had come into the pool. Ben took her other arm, and they helped her up the steps, the flimsy, wet robe clinging to her wiggling, bare, behind for all to see. And did they see. Mothers were covering the eyes of their children—especially the boys.

There were mumblings throughout the congregation—and a few giggles, before hands were slapped over eyes and mouths.

"Lord, have mercy!" came a cry from one of the sisters.

"Help us, Jesus!" came another.

"Oh, Father God!" came another.

"Be still, Satan! Be still!" another voice rang out.

"Umph! Humph! Humph!" came a groan.

The pianist began to play again, and the choir began to sing again: *Take me to the water.*

Sister Murray grabbed Conswella by the arm and trotted her down the back hallway—out of sight of the congregation now—but not out of Ben's. He stood as if in a trance, gazing down the hallway after the fleeing women. Forrest took him by the arm, led him to the other side of the pool and up the steps.

Conswella broke loose from Sister Murray and took off running down the hallway.

"Oh, Lord!" Sister Murray exclaimed when she realized Conswella was headed to a side door that led back into the sanctuary. She took off after the woman, her legs pumping, ample hips bouncing up and down.

Guess I'm getting my exercise today, but I've got to catch that heifer before she goes back into that sanctuary, Sister Murray thought. She picked up speed.

"What does that she-devil think she's doing?" Sister Murray asked herself. She had to stop the woman. She would probably be confined to her bed for the next three or four days, but she could not let that . . .

The door swung open just as Conswella reached it. It caught her smack-dab in the middle of her forehead, and down she went.

Sister Glenda Duncan walked through the door. "Oh, my Goodness!" she exclaimed. "What did I do?"

"You stopped a disaster, that's what you did. Thank you."

"Oh, my Lord, I might have killed her."

Sister Murray touched her hand to the side of Conswella's neck. "Unfortunately, she's still breathing. I guess you should have pushed that door just a little harder. Sister Duncan."

Sister Duncan chuckled. "Shame on you, Sister Murray."

Sister Murray grabbed Sister Conswella by both of her heels. "Come on. Help me get this hussy back to the Baptismal Room. She should come around in a few minutes."

Sister Duncan secured her handbag on her shoulder, put her hands under Conswella's armpits, and the two ladies started off down the hallway with the unconscious Conswella Cooper, First St. Marks newest convert, swinging between them.

Chapter Twenty-Nine

"Why didn't you put a slip on that gal?" asked one of the mothers.

The Deaconesses and the Mothers of the church had converged on Sister Murray after service.

"I did put one on her. She excused herself. Said she had to go to the rest room. I found the slip hanging in one of the toilets. That heifer pulled it off, and that's not the half of it." Sister Murray said with her arms akimbo.

She proceeded to tell the other ladies what had happened after Sister Conswella left the baptismal pool and how Sister Duncan had come through the door leading back into the sanctuary just in time to stop the most humiliating thing that could have ever happened to their church.

"Sister Duncan was on her way to the rest room. Thank God for her weak bladder."

"Thank God," echoed some of the other ladies.

"What is that child trying to do?" one of the other mothers asked.

"Guess," said another.

"She's after somebody, and whoever it is, he doesn't have a chance," one of the other ladies said, shaking her head.

"Help him, Jesus!" came a plea.

"She always sashays all the way down to the front bench, right in front of the pulpit, wearing those tight, bob-tailed dresses, so I guess we've got a good idea who she's after," said one of the mothers.

"Well, I hope which ever one it is has sense enough to run as fast as his legs can carry him, because that young she-devil has trouble written all over her," one of the deaconesses said.

"Did you all see all that wiggling she was doing up in that pool?" another sister asked.

"Couldn't help but see it if you had your eyes open," another of the ladies offered.

"I'm just glad my husband's already dead and buried or I'd have to kill him," another sister said.

"I hope I don't have to kill Brother Miles," said Sister Evelyn Miles.

"She's trouble," said Mother McDonald. "But we have an even more serious problem on our hands, ladies."

"Yeah, the preacher's new demands. I'm not buying," said one of the deaconesses.

"Neither am I," echoed Mother McDonald.

"Me neither."

"Me neither."

"Me neither."

And the negative remarks went on and on.

The mothers and the members of the deaconess board of First St. Marks were not adhering to the new directive that had been issued from the pulpit that morning.

Chapter Thirty

Ben and Forrest stood at the front door of the church bidding the parishioners goodbye. The morning services seemed to have gotten back on track after the baptism fiasco.

Sister Cooper had paraded down the center aisle in a sky-blue dress—that almost covered the breasts that had been trying to burst out of her baptismal attire—approximately forty-five minutes after her baptism. She wore matching blue shoes, a blue hat, and dangled a small blue purse from the middle finger of her right hand.

She also sported a good-sized bump in the middle of her forehead that the extra make-up she had applied was not quite successful in hiding.

She was still confused as to how the bump on her forehead had gotten there. She had awakened on a bench in the Baptismal Dressing Room. When she asked Sister Murray what had happened, she was told that she had run into a door.

Yes, she remembered running down the hallway, trying to get back into the sanctuary, so she could continue shouting, so the congregation could see what a good Christian woman she had become. How her baptism had washed her clean of any sins that might have been lurking in her.

Wasn't that what they said? That the water would wash away your sins? She thought if those nosy, little old biddies saw her shouting—in the spirit—that might stop all the whispering behind her back. And it might also help her with her plan to nab the pastor. Yes, she was putting on an act, but she had a job to do.

Maybe she should have waited until she put her clothes back on before coming back into the sanctuary, but she was on a roll. She wanted to show those wagging-tongued, holier-than-thou, good sisters of First St. Marks that she could get caught up in the spirit just like some of the rest of them.

She had almost made it, too. How in the hell had that door hit her in the face? She remembered reaching for it, but . . .

Oh, well, she'd figure all that out later.

She had even chosen a dress that was a bit longer to wear to church today. She thought now that she was being baptized, sealing her membership in this fine church, she had to dress more appropriately, thus, the added inch or two.

She just did not remember running into that door.

Ben had regained his composure after the episode in the pool, and had preached his heart out—although his mind was preoccupied, wondering what was taking Sister Cooper so long to get back into the sanctuary. She had missed quite a bit of his sermon.

But he had a job to do, and he could not allow himself to be swayed.

What he had done next was something he was not proud at all of doing. He had asked his congregation to increase their tithes from the usual ten percent to twenty. He had heard the groans of protests even after he had quoted the Bible verses he had been told to quote as a convincing tool—some of the same verses he had quoted to himself when trying to convince himself that he should not give back the blessings he had just received.

"That would be a slap in the good Lord's face," he told himself.

"Listen now, let us look at Malachi chapter three, verses ten and eleven: *'Bring ye all the tithes into the storehouse, that there may be meat in mine house, and prove me now herewith, saith the Lord of hosts, if I will not open you the windows of heaven, and pour you out a blessing, that there shall not be room enough to receive it.'* And we certainly don't want this brought down on our heads: "Malachi 3:8: *'Will a man rob God? Yet ye have robbed me in tithes and offerings.'* God said, if you pay your tithes and offerings, He will rebuke the devourer for your sakes. In other words, the Lord is saying, if you pay your tithes, He will step in to help you preserve the blessings he shall grant you by rebuking the thieves, the ungodly swindlers who try to rob you of those blessings. *'The enemy comes to steal and kill.'* In Second Corinthians chapter nine, verses six and seven, the Lord said, *'But this I say, He which soweth sparingly shall reap also sparingly; and he which soweth bountifully shall reap also bountifully.'* That tells us, brothers and sisters, that the more we give, the more blessings we shall receive. If we give a little, we are going to receive a little, but if we give a lot . . . Do you see how this thing works? If we tithe, brothers and sisters, He will pour so many financial blessings into our lives we will have a problem trying to deal with the increase. Wouldn't you like to have that problem? I certainly would."

"Well," said a sister from somewhere in the auditorium.

"Help us, Lord," cried another.

"Right now, Jesus," said another.

"When we tithe to our local church," Ben continued. "God supercharges his blessing over our finances. He brings out increases in all kinds of ways. I don't know about you, but that seems like a good deal to me. That is what happens when we tithe, sisters and brothers. But if we don't tithe, God will take our money blessings away from us. There are so many ways that can happen. The price of food goes up; interest rates go up; rent goes up; we get sick, and our insurance company refuses to pay the bill. All kinds of problems assail us. We have to protect ourselves, my brothers and sisters. And just think . . . if God blesses us so much and so fruitfully when we give ten percent, just think what He would do if we went beyond that designated amount and began to sow even greater seeds. We here at First St. Marks would like to challenge you to go beyond, sisters and brothers. Go beyond that ten percent. We would like for you to put that ten percent to rest, and increase your giving. Saints, wouldn't you like for your blessings to be doubled, tripled? I certainly would. We are asking you to increase your tithing from ten percent to twenty percent, and just watch and see how the Lord will move in your lives! How He will open that window even wider and pour out blessings that will be beyond your wildest dreams. Twenty percent, sisters and brothers, and watch the Lord show up and show out.

"That way, we can have some money in reserve, and when we need new lighting, a new furnace, new air conditioning, and whatever else that might come upon us, here at First St. Marks, we can do what needs to be done right away rather than have different fund raisers for our different needs. We take pride in our church, ladies and gentlemen. Let's go beyond with our tithes, and watch our blessings grow. God will do it, and don't let anyone tell you He won't. I am a witness that He will do it! Twenty percent, sisters and brothers. Give Him twenty percent and reap the benefits! Watch Him work in your lives! Watch Him work! Give, sit back and enjoy, and don't forget to give Him the glory! Hallelujah!"

Chapter Thirty-One

Much to his chagrin, Ben preached on, telling the congregation all the lies he had been instructed to tell them while using every Bible reference he could think of that spoke of tithing to corroborate what he was saying.

He had done it. Against his will, he had done what they had ordered him to do.

How many of his parishioners would go along with it? How many would not? How many would he lose? There were bound to be some who would leave the church, and he could not blame them really.

If they only knew what he was going through; if they only knew what was at stake with him.

But that was his problem, wasn't it?

He hated himself for doing this to his trusting flock, but what else could he do?

His last pitch to his congregation was that the expenditures of the church were increasing daily and that the church's income had to reflect that increase—which was true, really. Wasn't it? The cost of living was indeed increasing all over the land. Businesses were being asked to scale back, and the church was not exempt. Everybody was affected. So, he had not really lied. Except the church had no mortgage, so why did they need so much money?

They didn't really, but the members of the church did not know that.

But did the state of the economy warrant him asking his parishioners to double their tithes? Fifteen percent would have been much better. He had suggested to the committee that they ask for fifteen percent rather than twenty, but just like all of the other suggestions he had made to this body of men, it had been overruled.

Twenty percent had won out hands down.

Some of that money was going into the expenditure fund for the church as it should, but the bulk of it . . . He hated to think about where it was going.

He was the pastor of this Christian body of people, their leader. He was torn between his obligation to his congregation and his desire to remain pastor of this great church and benefit from all of the perks that came with the position—especially the last enormous one that had been added: the house. Davis had promised him the house. He was going to own Black Eden. It was going to be his. Davis also told him his salary was going to be increased after six months, so some of the increase in tithes was going into his own pockets.

But his conscience just did not seem to be able to compete with his increase.

But the woman, Sister Conswella, said it was all right. She told him to do it. She said she would gladly pay the increase to help her new church. If a new member was willing to do it, why wouldn't the old ones?

Yes, he had lied to these trusting people. Now he knew why he had been given the post, but it was too late to do anything about it. It was just too late. His hands were tied.

But was the house really going to be his? Deacon Davis had promised, but could he trust the man to come through on that promise? Could he one day actually own Black Eden? Was it really possible?

Where is your faith, Ben? He thought.

With God anything was possible. He knew that. But he wouldn't try to fool himself into believing God had a hand in what was happening at First St. Marks.

And now he had become a co-conspirator.

How could he ever make this right with God?

When Ben finished his sermon and sat down beside Forrest, he could feel his son's eyes boring through him.

"What in the world . . .?" Forrest whispered to his father while looking at him with utter disbelief on his face. "Dad—"

Then the pianist began playing the song for *opening the doors of the church.*

Thank God, Ben thought, as Forrest rose and went to the pulpit.

≈≈≈

"I know what you're doing."

The words brought Ben out of his reverie. He looked into the face of Mother McDonald. She had not spoken to him for quite some time now. He wished she had not today.

"God is going to punish you, and punish you good," she continued. She brushed on past them and out the front door.

Forrest looked at his father. "It's the money. She's talking about the money. Doubling the tithes . . .? Why did you do it, Dad?"

"I won't pay it."

They both turned to face a frail-looking woman who stood before them. She looked to be in her late seventies. She wore a black suit and a black hat that looked decent, but about a decade out of style. She just looked at them for a moment, her eyes cold, piercing, and unrelenting.

"I voted for you. Now I wish I hadn't," the woman continued. She walked off, thought better of it, turned and walked back over to them. "I'm not paying no extra tithes, and I'm not leaving my church either. I won't give the devil that satisfaction! We're going to be praying on this. You'd better watch what you're doing . . ." She squared her shoulders and said the next word with total disdain. ". . . *Pastor*, because somebody is surely watching you."

They watched her stalk off toward the front door.

"This is bad," Forrest whispered.

"I had to do it," Ben said, his voice barely above a whisper.

"No, you didn't."

"The devil sure is busy around this place lately," this comment came from another of St Marks' mothers as she passed by the two ministers.

"Loose him, Satan!" another woman shouted as she passed them, then almost ran on out the door.

"You've messed up, Dad. You've really messed up," Forrest whispered to his father.

Ben looked blankly at his son for a moment.

Deacon Davis appeared before them. "Good job." Davis reached out his hand to Ben; Ben took it, and the two men shook hands. Davis turned to Forrest, gave him a curt nod, smiled, and then walked off toward the front door.

Forrest turned to his father, a mixture of confusion, anger and concern on his face.

Chapter Thirty-Two

Ben and Forrest sat on the veranda just outside the dining room. They had finished their Sunday afternoon dinner, and, as had become their custom, had adjourned to the veranda for their afternoon tea. Mrs. Barber had served them and then gone back into the house.

"Why?" Forrest asked.

"I can't. . . I'm not at liberty to—" Ben began.

"Don't give me that crap, Dad! Tell me what's going on!" Forrest had lost all patience with his father. He had tried to talk with him at dinner to no avail. He could sense that Ben wanted to talk, to open up, but Forrest could see the fear in his eyes. His father was deathly afraid of something, and he had to find out what that something was.

"That was not you talking in that church today. You wouldn't have done such a thing. That was not the preacher, the father, if you will, that I know. That was somebody else: I don't know that person! I don't like that person! I want my father back! What have those men, that committee from the church that has been invading our home for the past month, done to you?

What have they done, Dad? What are they holding over your head to make you outright lie to God's people?"

"I, I can't talk about it" Ben began,

"Stop it! Stop it with the 'I can't!' You can do whatever you want to do. You are a grown man. No other man should be able to dictate to you how you should live your life, how you should conduct yourself, especially in the church, standing at the pulpit, for God's sake!" He stopped a moment, wiped at his face. When he spoke again, his voice was a bit calmer. "You asked our parishioners to increase their tithes from ten percent to twenty. Why? What's going on, Dad? I need to know."

"I didn't want to do it."

"Then why did you?"

"I had to, Son. I had to."

"No, you didn't!"

"I can't talk about it. It's secret."

Forrest leapt to his feet. "Secret, my ass!" he shouted.

Ben looked at his son, aghast. Forrest had never taken that tone with him. "Son—" he began.

"I'm sorry, Dad. I'm sorry. This is just getting to me." Forrest turned and started for the door.

"He's going to give me the mansion," Ben yelled after him.

Forrest turned back around. "What?"

"Davis is going to give me the mansion." Ben made a grand gesture. "This is all going to be ours, Son. Black Eden is going to be ours."

"Dad, he can't do that."

"Yes, yes he can. Davis said there is no clause in the will that says the house cannot be deeded to someone else. The Board of Trustees can do it. They're working on it now. And she told me to do it. She said it was all right."

"Who said it was all right?"

"Sister Cooper. She said—"

Forrest was incredulous. "You did it because of Davis and a worthless promise, and because that woman told you to do it? I don't believe you, Dad. I can't believe you would stoop so low as to fleece your flock for personal gain. Even if Davis does manage to steal the church's house and give it to you, I just can't see you doing that, Dad. And the woman . . . well, Dad, I just don't know what to say about her. I can't believe you!" he turned and stormed into the house.

Ben looked after his son, with tears welling in his eyes. What was he going to do? What could he do to change things now that he had done this terrible thing to his congregation?

He had no idea.

Forrest went upstairs to his room, slammed the door behind him, walked over to the bed, and fell on his knees beside it.

"Father . . ." he began.

Chapter Thirty-Three

The next day, Forrest went to see Mother McDonald. He had come to see her out of sheer desperation. He had to talk with somebody, and he thought she would be the perfect person to give him some insight as to what was going on with his father, and why his father seemed afraid to even talk with him, his own son.

They're doing it again," Mother McDonald said.

She and Forrest sat at her kitchen table drinking tea.

"Doing what, Mother McDonald? Just what are they doing?" Forrest asked. He had to know, and then maybe he could find some way to help his father.

"Your father . . . they've gotten to him. They've turned him into their puppet. They are controlling him, having him help them do their dirty work. The directive from the pulpit yesterday was appalling. That was not your father talking; it was Davis and his cronies. They want more money to line their pockets."

"Stealing from the church," Forrest interjected.

"That's right. Most of the people will see right through their agenda. Most of us won't pay it. But some will, and that's what they are banking on. That Davis is a real scoundrel."

"And they've persuaded my father to help them steal from the church. This is so unreal"

"Somehow they have convinced him to join forces with them."

"I knew they were up to no good. I knew it. All of the secret meetings."

"The secret society of First St. Marks."

"That's not good."

"No, it isn't."

"How do they get away with it, Mother McDonald?"

"By doing just what they are doing with your father. If they have the preacher in their back pockets, they're home free."

"And they are holding the position, the huge salary, the mansion, and the car over his head, right?"

"All of the perks."

"He says Davis has promised to give him the house."

"What?" Mother McDonald looked at him in puzzlement. "He can't do that. That house belongs to the church. But that scoundrel and that crooked lawyer he has just might find a way to do it," Mother McDonald admitted.

"My father is so afraid of losing everything. And I think he would do just about anything for that house. He's so enamored with it. He looks at it sometimes as if he worships it."

"That house is cursed. You should have listened to me—"

"And taken the parsonage. I know." Forrest said interrupting her. "I should have been more persistent. I should have insisted that we take the parsonage. It would have been a battle, but I might have gotten him to listen. I just don't know, Mother McDonald. Now, it's as if he's losing his mind."

"He's torn between doing the right thing and what they are telling him to do. And of course, he's afraid of losing his new status in life."

"It's not worth it, Mother McDonald, but I can't make him see that."

"Of course, you can't, because he doesn't want to see it, and they know this. They have a way of coercing people into doing their will. Take Reverend and Mrs. Williams for instance. They were good people. We liked him as a pastor. He was trying to clean up things around First St. Marks. Davis and his crew tried to break him, but he was too strong for them, a strong-willed man who was determined he was not going to let them dictate to him about how he should run his church. One day, they were gone, the whole family. Only God knows where. They just disappeared. No one ever heard from them again. The children didn't even say goodbye to their friends at the church. Children usually talk. I didn't see anything. I didn't feel as if anything bad had happened to them. They just vanished. I wished them God speed. God didn't show me anything about them. He shows me things in my dreams, you know."

"Yes, ma'am, I remember. That's why I came to see you."

"I'm glad you did." She paused a moment, her expression grave. "Then there were poor Reverend Simms and his wife. Simms went even farther. Despite what Davis and his committee had instructed him to do, he was determined to stop the corruption. He told them he was going tell the people the truth: that God wanted us to stop tithing. He said he was going to let the church-body know that we were not under the law anymore, that we were now under *grace,* and grace did not demand that we tithe, that free-will offerings were what we should be giving, and he had scriptures to back up his statement."

"Corinthians 9:7. *'Every man according as he purposeth in his heart, so let him give; not grudgingly, or of necessity; for the Lord loveth a cheerful giver.'"*

"That's right. He said ministers have not been interpreting that passage properly," said Mother McDonald.

"They want the money to keep rolling in," Forrest interjected.

Mother McDonald nodded her head. "Pastor Simms was determined to set the record straight as he saw it, and Davis was determined to not let that happen. I don't know what all they did to that poor man, but he was such a tortured soul in the end, and that was a shame, because he had been so vibrant, such a good teacher of the word. We all loved him and his wife. They seemed to be perfect for what we needed at First St. Marks. Then we saw him changing right before our eyes. Then he finally broke, went completely mad, they said. They said he drowned his wife in the pond in back of the mansion, and then hanged himself on the hanging tree."

"Oh, my God!" Forrest exclaimed.

"You didn't know?"

"No, I heard they died, but I hadn't heard the details."

"They're trying to keep it as quiet as they can. They did it, you know."

Forrest looked at her, confused. "Somebody killed them?"

"It's a mystery. But whether they did it or not, they were still responsible. They just would not let up. He couldn't take it anymore."

"You're talking about Deacon Davis and his followers, of course."

"You bet I am. That so-called committee of theirs. They just won't quit. No matter what happens. They just won't quit. Oh, they were acting all innocent, as if they really cared when Pastor Simms and his wife were found dead at the mansion. But they couldn't fool me. I knew. I saw it."

"You saw them being murdered in your dreams?"

"No. No, I saw the hammering, the intimidation, the threats, the brainwashing!" She held the sides of her head as if trying to ward off a migraine. "They just kept pushing, and pushing until he . . . until he had to escape. But I still don't believe he killed his wife. He loved her too much."

"So, you think Davis and his followers, for lack of a better word to call them, murdered those people?"

"I wouldn't doubt it for one minute. They're up to no good, you know."

"But Davis is the chairman of First St. Marks' Deacon Board."

"That's right. Right on top where he has access to everybody and everything."

"But if the church knows what he is doing, why is he allowed to remain in that position and continue with his terrifying activities?"

"He is allowed to continue his ungodly ways because everybody who is anybody around First St. Marks is in cahoots with him."

"My father . . . Yesterday. . ."

She nodded her head. "They have gotten to him."

"But he's an honest man, a decent man."

"I'm sure he was."

"He said the woman told him to do it."

"What woman?"

"The Cooper woman, our new convert."

"Good, Lord. He's listening to her? That woman is up to no good. He'd better stay as far away from that piece of trash as he possibly can."

They just sat for a moment, Forrest trying to digest all the things Mother McDonald had just told him,

Forrest finally broke the silence. "So, it's all about the money. The big jump in tithes that my father, the minister, is encouraging . . ."

"Yes, once they have the minister in their clutches . . ." Mother McDonald left the sentence dangling, as her eyes bore into his. "They seem to have succeeded."

"They have been coming by the house as much as three times a week. They shut themselves up in the library with my father. I've listened at the door a few times and heard parts of their conversations. Mother McDonald, he's a total wreck when he leaves those meetings, and he just clams up, refuses to talk. He has wanted First St. Marks for so many years, and now that he has it, I believe he would do just about anything to hold onto it. What he did yesterday certainly proves that. I didn't think I would ever live to see the day when my father would compromise his position as a pastor—his relationship with God, if you will—for temporal pleasures that shall soon pass away. He knows better, Mother McDonald. He knows better."

"I know. And I know it's hard for you to see him like this, but it's done, and it will only get worse."

"I have to make him see that." Forrest looked at Mother McDonald with pleading eyes. "How can I make him see that, Mother McDonald?"

She just looked at him and shook her head.

"Tell me something else, Mother McDonald, why don't they hire members from First St Marks to work at the mansion, rather than non-members?"

"They don't want the things that go on at that house leaked back to the church. They know how to cover their behinds."

"They seem to have thought of everything."

"Oh, they know what they're doing all right. I just wish I could tell you more, but my dreams are so befuddled of late. I'm having such a hard time trying to decipher them. There's so much going on at the house and at the church. First St. Marks was such a good church once. Until Gaston Davis showed his face. Things began to unravel then, and they have been on a decline ever since."

"All for money . . ."

"Yes. I've seen money changing hands so many times. I suspect Davis is pocketing a good deal of the church's money to help finance his upcoming mayoral campaign. I can't prove it, of course, but I just know deep down in my soul. With the members, those who decide to pay the increase, of course, paying twenty percent instead of the usual ten, Davis will have more money to pocket."

"Stealing from the church to finance his campaign . . . And they are using my father to help them do it. My God!"

"The house, the car, the big salary are all good incentives." Mother McDonald made a futile gesture.

"How could he refuse all that? Right?"

"They can make it look so good."

"My father has never been a weak man."

"They say 'everyone has his price,' but, then, some people are stronger than others, like Pastor Williams and Pastor Simms. Oh, my Lord, they tried, and look where it got them."

"But my father . . . He has always been a good Christian man. How could he allow himself to be manipulated that way?"

"They can be most persuasive."

"I have to do something. I have to help him, but I don't know what to do," Forrest said, totally frustrated.

"There's not much you can do. He's the minister," Mother McDonald offered.

"I know, and I'm just the lowly assistant. Davis delights in reminding me of my status at the church. Sometimes I just want to punch him, Mother McDonald, to just put my fist right through his big mouth."

Mother McDonald chuckled. "But, of course, you can't do that."

"No, I can't, but there's no harm in wishing."

"I have to admit, I'd like to see that myself."

They both chuckled, and then Forrest's face clouded again. "I can't just stand by and watch while my father is being browbeaten into---"

Mother McDonald held up a staying hand. "Wait, a minute." she said interrupting him. "There just might be something I can do to help."

"What is it? Just tell me what I can do to help. I'll do anything."

"I think I'd better do this on my own. But there is something you can do, Son. You can pray. "God is still on the throne."

.

Chapter Thirty-Four

Forrest pulled up to the house, punched the remote on his visor, and the garage door went up. He was pulling the car into the garage opening when he noticed Mrs. Barber coming through the front door dragging a large suitcase behind her. He stopped the car, hopped out of it, and hurried over to her. She was coming down the steps now, the suitcase bouncing along behind her.

"Mrs. Barber, where are you going?" he asked, reaching out his hand to take hold of the luggage.

"I can't stay here any longer, Reverend Thomas." Without breaking her stride, she rushed on past him.

He caught up with her and took her by the arm. "What do you mean you can't stay here any longer? What happened?"

"Ask your father." She pulled her arm free and hurried on down the walkway.

"What's happening?"

A taxi pulled up into the driveway. Forrest watched as the trunk went up and the driver got out of the car. The man looked fleetingly at Forrest then, apparently deciding the woman was his fare, turned his attention to Mrs. Barber. He walked swiftly around the car, opened the back door, helped the woman into the car, closed the door, picked up the piece of luggage from the pavement, walked around to the back of the car, and put the luggage inside. He closed the trunk, got back into the car, and drove off down the street.

"What in the world?" Forrest watched until the car's taillights were out of sight. He got back into his car, pulled it into the garage, leaped out of it and rushed through the door leading onto the back hallway. He went on through the kitchen and the dining room into the living room.

"Dad?" he called. There was no answer. "Dad?" he called again. There was still no answer.

"Where is he?" Forrest whispered to himself. He turned and raced up the stairs. "Dad?" he called again as he crested the stairs.

He stopped. He heard sounds coming from. . . From where were the sounds coming? He walked on down the hallway. His father's bedroom. The sounds were coming from his father's bedroom. What was going on?

Then he heard it—a scream, a man's voice. His father was screaming.

"Oh, my God, what's happening?" Forrest ran the few yards down the hallway to his father's room. Someone was hurting his father. He knew who it was. Those hypocrites: the mighty Deacon Davis and his crew. What were they doing to his father?

He heard another scream, louder this time.

He would kill them.

Forrest grabbed the knob, tried to turn it, and pushed. The door was locked. He began pounding on the door. "Open this door, you bastards! What are you doing to my father? Open this door. Now!"

He continued his pounding for a moment then pulled his cell phone from his pocket. "I'm calling the police! Do you hear me in there? I'm calling the police!"

The door opened, and Conswella Cooper stepped out of the room. She was barefoot, wearing one of Ben's robes, a snide smile playing on her lips.

"Hi," she said.

"What? What's going on? What are you doing here, in my father's bedroom?

She chuckled. "What does it look like I'm doing? Your father wasn't screaming because he was in pain. He'll probably sleep like a baby tonight."

Forrest gaped at her. "Oh, my God!" he moaned. He raced into his father's room, stepping over discarded clothes that were strewn about the floor.

Ben sat on the side of the bed. He was trying to cover his nakedness with the disheveled bedclothes.

"Dad, what are you doing?" Forrest asked.

"I don't know. I, I . . ." Ben's voice trailed off.

"You don't know?" Forrest rushed over to the bed and yanked the bedclothes off his father's naked frame.

Ben tried to cover his private parts with his hands, shame and befuddlement on his face.

"You don't know?" Forrest screamed.

Conswella's laughter from the doorway had him whirling about. The woman turned and strolled off down the hallway as if she belonged there.

Forrest raced after her, grabbed her arm, turning her to face him. "What do you think you're doing?"

She smiled at him. "I'm going to make Ben and me some coffee. Would you like a cup?"

"Woman, are you crazy?" He pointed toward his father's bedroom. "You get yourself dressed and get out of this house! Now!"

She looked at him and then down at his hand on her arm. "You're hurting me."

"If you don't get out of this house right now, I'm going to show you what hurt is, woman!" Forrest said.

That snide smile remained on her lips, and her voice never lost its calmness. "I guess your father hasn't gotten around to telling you? I'm moving in. Ben and I are getting married. We became engaged earlier today." She held up her left hand, showing him an antique gold and diamond ring on her ring finger.

Forrest looked at her hand, aghast. "That's my mother's ring."

"You can call me Mommy if you'd like."

He grabbed her left hand, and began yanking at the ring. "Take it off! You take my mother's ring off your finger right now or I'll. . ."

"Or you'll what? You take your hands off me, or I'm going to call the police." She wretched her arm from his grasp, turned, and went on down the hallway.

Dr. Mildred Dumàs

Chapter Thirty-Five

Forrest stood, stunned. His father was going to marry the woman? He could not believe his ears. He could not let that happen. He would not. He couldn't. "Oh, dear God, help us," he moaned.

He rushed back into his father's bedroom. His father still sat on the side of the bed, a sheet thrown haphazardly over the lower part of his nude body now. He looked up, shame and guilt written all over his face.

"I love her," Ben said.

Forrest began snatching up the woman's clothes. "You're disgusting."

"I'm going to marry her."

"Over my dead body!" Forrest shifted Conswella's clothes to his left arm, and then began picking up his father's clothes, throwing them at him. "Put on your clothes!" He hurried from the room, his arms loaded with Conswella's clothes and shoes.

He raced down the hallway, reaching the top of the stairs just as Conswella reached the bottom. He threw the clothes down the stairs. They landed in a heap near the bottom, some on the stairs and some on the floor. "Put on your clothes and get out of this house!"

She smiled up at him. "I'll go when your father tells me to do so."

"You're going now! Of your own accord, or I'm going to throw you out!"

"Son, she's going to be my wife. You have no right."

Forrest turned to see his father hurrying down the hallway. He now wore a robe and house slippers.

"I have every right. You're my father, and you have apparently taken leave of your senses. I have to protect you, if I have to have you committed to do it."

"Protect me from what? The woman I love?" Ben went past Forrest on down the stairs.

Conswella stood, looking up at her new fiancé as he came down the steps toward her.

When Ben stepped down into the room, Conswella took his face in her hands, brought it down to meet hers, and kissed him full on the mouth, her eyes open, fastened on Forrest who still stood at the top of the stairs.

Ben took both of her hands in his. "Maybe you should go now. I'll call you later."

Forrest walked off down the upstairs hallway, his mind racing. He could not believe what he was seeing. He had to do something. But what could he do?

Conswella and Ben picked up her clothes. Ben handed her the pieces he had gathered. She took them, moved away from him, and started up the stairs. As she stepped onto the upstairs hallway, she spotted Forrest a few yards away—pacing, his head down. He looked up. She untied the belt from around her waist and let the front of the robe fall open. She wore nothing underneath.

Forrest rushed up to her, yanked the robe together, and retied the belt. "I'm not interested, you filthy slut!"

She smiled at him, went on past him, and started to open the door to Ben's bedroom.

Forrest grabbed her arm. "You can dress in the guest room across the hall." He marched her across the hallway to another room.

He opened the door and stood aside for her to enter. She brushed up against him as she passed—the smile still pasted on her lips. Just as she went through the door, she untied the belt from about her waist—again--pulled the robe from her shoulders, and let it fall down around her ankles.

She stood just inside the door, her nude body facing him, still smiling, her eyes glued to his face. He kicked the robe on into the room, and slammed the door.

Her shrilling laughter echoed in his ears as he hurried off down the hallway toward the stairs. Just as he neared the stairs, his father stepped onto the hallway. He stopped and just looked at Ben, shaking his head in total disgust and confusion.

"Are you crazy? Do you know the kind of stir this would cause at the church?"

"She just stopped by to talk. We were in the parlor laughing and talking, and then she started kissing me, and somehow we ended up in my bedroom."

"Somehow? Somehow, Dad?"

"Just stop, will you? Where is she?" the older man asked.

"She's getting dressed, so she can leave this house. How long has this been going on, Dad? How long have you been sleeping with that woman here in the church's house?"

"This was the first time."

"How can I believe that in light of what just happened?"

"Believe what you want. And stop interrogating me as if I've committed a crime. I don't have to answer to you."

"No, you don't, but you do have to answer to God. And, yes, in His eyes, you have committed a crime."

Ben stormed off down the hallway.

Forrest caught up with him. "You're a minister, Dad. Act like it, for God's sake!"

Conswella emerged from the room fully dressed. The two men stopped, their eyes pivoting toward her.

She walked up to Ben, a broad smile on her face. "Are you all right, darling?"

"I'm fine," Ben said.

She took his hand in hers and squeezed it. Then she kissed him full on the lips. "See you later." She let her eyes roll over Forrest's face as she went past him down the hallway toward the stairs.

"I'll show you out," Forrest said.

"I'll show her out. She's my guest," Ben said.

"You just wait right here! We need to talk!" Forrest commanded his father. He fell in step beside Conswella.

"But she's my guest," Ben insisted.

"I will show her out!" Forrest shouted. "Wait right here," he finished in a calmer voice.

Ben opened his mouth to say something else, thought better of it, and nodded his head.

"I know my way out," Conswella said.

"I'm sure you do. It has been barely more than a month since you met my father, and you're already in love and engaged to be married. That says something, Ms. Cooper. Yes, it does."

"One never knows when or where love is going to strike, does one? Haven't you ever heard of *love at first sight*," she said.

"We both know that's a bunch of bull in this case, don't we? What are you after, Ms. Cooper? What do you want?"

They continued down the hallway. Ben stood looking after them until they reached the top of the stairs.

"I've already found it. Remember?" She flashed her engagement ring, again, for him to see.

"Is it money? How much? How much would it take to buy you off, Ms. Cooper?"

"I'm not after money, Pastor Forrest."

"Then what do you want?"

She was silent.

"How long has this been going on? A week? Two?" Forrest asked as he led the way down the stairs.

"Long enough," Conswella said.

"He's more than twice your age."

"So? Maybe I like older men."

"When they have something that you want, right? Are you thinking about taking over this house? If so, you can think again. That will never happen as long as I'm alive."

"Don't tempt me," she said as they reached the bottom of the stairs.

Forrest continued as if she had not spoken as he led the way through other parts of the house. "The title of First Lady of First St. Marks? Is that what you want? That, too, will never happen as long as I have breath in my body."

She chuckled. "You're awfully sure of yourself, aren't you?"

"And I don't think the members of First St. Marks would allow that to happen either, Ms. Cooper. I think they would see right through you, just as I do."

"If I'm married to the pastor, I automatically become First Lady."

"And we would all be thrown out of this house on our behinds, because the members of the church would know my father was totally out of his mind, and his reign as pastor of First St. Marks would be immediately terminated! What's your game, Ms. Cooper?"

"Game?" She looked at him, her expression innocent.

"The man is a minister!"

"I know. And I'm about to become the minister's wife: The First Lady of First St. Marks Missionary Baptist Church! I suggest you get used to the idea!" She smirked at him.

"Not if I can help it!"

"Your daddy's a big boy. He doesn't need your permission."

"It will never happen," he said, his eyes challenging her.

"We shall see. Won't we?"

"Where's your car?"

"Out back. Your father told me to park it there just in case . . . You know how some folk love to talk."

"Well, you and my father have certainly given them something to talk about now. Just wait until this little episode hits the fan."

He led the way through the kitchen, down a back hallway to a door that led to the back yard. He flung the door open and looked at her. "Don't ever come back here again."

"I think that's for Ben to decide. He loves me. We're engaged." She held up her left hand for him to see the ring again, chuckled, and then went on out the door.

Chapter Thirty-Six

Forrest slammed the door behind her and went back down the hallway to the kitchen. He spotted his father at the counter pouring a cup of coffee.

"You want a cup?" Ben asked.

"No, Dad. I really don't feel like socializing. Let's go into the den, shall we?" He led the way to the den and held the door open for his father to enter. Ben sat on the sofa; Forrest sat on a chair across from him.

"I don't believe you, Dad. You could lose everything. We could lose everything. Do you have any idea what the consequences are for what you are doing?"

"I love her, and she loves me. We're getting married. There's nothing wrong with that. I'm a widower, and she's a single woman. Preachers get married every day."

"Not to that kind of woman. You can't bring her up into First St. Marks proclaiming her to be your wife, the new First Lady. Do you know what kind of scandal that would cause?"

"Why should it? People can't tell me whom I should or should not marry."

"Don't be naïve, Dad! Anybody can look at that woman and tell she's nothing short of a street walker."

"That's not true! She just likes to dress nicely. She's going to start wearing more suitable clothes. We talked about that. I don't know what she has done in the past. That's all behind her now. She has become a good Christian lady, and we're going to get married and start a new life together."

"Your marrying that woman would destroy our relationship with the church, Dad. Can't you see that? Marrying a woman who is young enough to be your daughter, a woman that no one has ever seen or heard of before she came strutting up into the church a few Sundays ago . . . Dad, it would be a disgrace."

"Why? Men marry younger women all the time."

"Not when they look, dress, and act like hooker material. Everyone can see that except you, Dad."

"Stop talking about her like she's some kind of disease. She's a nice young lady. Whatever she was before, she's not that person anymore. She's a Christian lady now."

"You can keep telling yourself that, Dad, but deep down inside, you know I'm right."

"You're just thinking about your mother. You don't think any woman could ever replace her."

"Certainly not a woman of Ms. Cooper's character. And this is not about Mom. This is about you and the biggest mistake of your life that you seem to be determined to make."

"Other men marry younger women, Son. Why can't I?"

"Why? Think about it, Dad. You're not just any man. You are a minister, a man of the cloth. You have to carry yourself in that manner. Suppose you were counseling a couple contemplating marriage at the church. Suppose they had just met. Suppose she was an older woman and he was a much younger man. Suppose she was fixed in life, and he was struggling just trying to make ends meet. What would you tell them? What would you tell the woman?"

"I'd tell her if she loved him to go ahead and marry him. You can't just judge people because of their circumstances, Son."

Forrest chuckled. "Yeah, I'll bet you would tell her to go ahead and marry him. And, of course, you would tell an older man to go ahead and marry a younger woman whom you knew was just after what she could get out of him."

"It would be their choice in the end."

"Of course, it would." Forrest hit the table with his fist as hard as he could. "The woman has an agenda!" he screamed at his father. "She just met you, and is already madly in love with you? That should tell you something. Don't be a fool! She wants something! Can't you see that?"

"Are you jealous, Son? Do you want her for yourself?"

"If I wanted her, I could have her, Dad. She exposed herself to me, in the upstairs hallway, just a few minutes ago."

Ben leapt to his feet. "You're lying!" he screamed.

"She tried to tempt me, Dad."

"Stop it! Just stop it! She loves me!"

"She doesn't love you, Dad. She's after what she can get out of you."

"Stop lying. You just want her for yourself."

"That's ridiculous."

"Then why haven't you married your fiancée, Sylvia. What's the holdup?"

"You, Dad! You are the hold up. I'm so busy trying to untangle this mess you've gotten into with Deacon Davis and those other hypocrites, and now this! I don't have time to think about my own life, because I'm too busy trying to save yours, and it's driving me crazy!"

"You don't have to worry about me! I can take care of myself! Now let me alone! I'm going to marry her, and that's the end of it!"

"That would be the end of you, believe me. What do you think is going to happen when people find out what happened here today, Dad?"

"It was just a moment of weakness. No one will have to know."

"Mrs. Barber was leaving when I drove up," Forrest offered.

Ben stood, his eyes cast down. "I'm sorry about that."

"How could you do it, Dad? Carrying on with that woman right here in the house, in front of our housekeeper. My, God! If Mrs. Barber tells just one person, we're doomed. You're a minister, for God's sake. Act like it. How are you going to minister to others, if you don't follow the doctrine yourself? Your own teachings?"

"I'm human!"

"Is that your excuse? You're human? Dad, what were you thinking?"

"It just happened."

"Things don't just happen, Dad. People make things happen. You know that. You preach it all the time. You let people know that they are responsible for the decisions they make in their personal lives and in their walk with God. You're lusting after the flesh, Dad. You've stepped into the Devil's domain. You've brought shame on us—our good name. You've brought shame to our new home. How could you? Or have you no shame?" This might just be too bitter of a pill for some people to swallow, Dad. This and the plea for the people to double their tithes. What has gotten into you, Dad? You're not the man I once knew."

"I don't have to stand here and listen to all of this ridicule. I'm a grown man, your father, by the way, and you're right, I make my own decisions! And I have made my decision about this matter." He started for the door. "I'm going to bed."

He stormed from the room.

Forrest followed close behind him. "'*Do not be deceived. Bad company ruins good morals.*' 1 Corinthians 15:33. '*Flee from sexual immorality. Every other sin a person commits is outside the body, but the sexually immoral person sins against his own body.*' 1 Corinthians 6:18.'"

They started up the stairs, Ben still in front, Forrest following—still reciting Bible verses. "'. . . *abstain from sexual immorality; that each one of you know how to control his own body in holiness and honor . . .*' 1 Thessalonians 4:3 and 5. '*To set the mind on the flesh is death, but to set the mind on the Spirit is life and peace.*'

Romans 8:6. *'If your right eye causes you to sin, tear it out and throw it away. For it is better that you lose one of your members than that your whole body be thrown into hell.'''*

They went on down the upstairs hallway, Ben still in the lead, Forrest still reciting Bible verses. *"'But each person is tempted when he is lured and enticed by his own desire. Then desire gives birth to sin, and sin brings forth death.' James 1:14-15. 'If you love me, you will keep my commandments.' John 14:15. 'You shall not commit adultery.' Exodus 20:14.'''*

Ben whirled about, his hand on his bedroom door, his face a mask of rage *"'Nevertheless, to avoid fornication, let every man have his own wife!' 1 Corinthians 7:2!'''* He went on into the room and slammed the door in Forrest's face.

Forrest fell against the door, his head resting on his arms. *"'. . . and let the marriage bed be undefiled . . .'''* he whispered to himself.

He fisted his hand, and beat lightly on the door, as tears coursed down his face.

He could not believe his father was being so stupid. He could not believe what was happening to their lives. That his father was about to make the biggest mistake of his life, and it seemed he was powerless to stop that from happening.

He could not believe the change that had come over his father in just a couple of months.

But, then, maybe he could. Mother McDonald had told them the house was cursed.

Chapter Thirty-Seven

"You can't do it, Dad! You're talking like a fool!" Forrest was beside himself with rage.

They sat at the dining room table, Ben at the head and Forrest at the other end, beginning their day as usual as if it was just another day. But they both knew it was not—not after what had happened the night before.

The woman, and his father's defiled bed.

And not only that, but their cook slash housekeeper had walked out on them because of the woman and his father's sinfulness.

What were they going to tell Davis and the others? What was Mrs. Barber going to tell them? She had to give some reason why she quit her job. He dreaded to think about what was going to happen behind this shameful incident. What kind of salvation did they have?

None of which he could think.

How were they going to clean up this mess?

He did not think they could.

They were resuming their conversation from the night before. Forrest had tried to let it rest, but found that he just could not do so, not with the enormity of it all. Not after his father had stated that he still planned to marry the woman.

"I love her." Ben said for what Forrest thought must have been the thousandth time.

"Is that all you can say? You love her? You sound like a broken record, Dad! What in the world did that woman do to you? Just think about what you're saying, will you? Think about what you are doing! Stop and think!"

"I don't need to think about it anymore. It's settled, and you might as well get used to the idea."

"She's young enough to be your daughter, Dad! The woman is using you."

"What's age got to do with it?"

"Maybe everything in this case. Maybe she's banking on you being old and senile, an old fool, easy prey, easy to manipulate." Forrest paused a moment and looked at his father's blank face. "And it looks like she's doing just that—unless you come to your senses."

Forrest had cooked since they did not have a cook anymore. He understood why Mrs. Barber had left. His father's behavior with that woman was atrocious. He was acting like a complete idiot. That young woman had him so confused, he didn't know whether he was going or coming.

How could he even think he was in love with such a person as she?

"How long has this been going on, Dad? Have you been sneaking that woman into this house while I've been away? Late at night when I'm asleep?"

"I don't have to sneak and do anything. This is my house, too, even more so than yours. I am the senior pastor."

"And that's all the more reason why you can't have that woman, or any other woman, in this house! In your bed! This is the church's house."

"This is where I live."

"In the church's house!"

"We're going to be married," Ben protested.

"But you're not married!"

"We will be soon, and this will be my house soon, too, and my wife will be living here with me, and if you don't like it, maybe you need to find someplace else to live!"

"I guess I'll have to do that if you continue with your plans to marry her. But since you are not married yet, in the meantime, you're going to just shack up with her here, in the church's house?"

"Stop saying that! I told you that was a mistake. It won't happen again, and no one has to know about last night."

Forrest looked at him aghast. "I know. You know. Mrs. Barber knows! He pointed upward. God knows! And how do you know it won't happen again, Dad? You couldn't stop it from happening last night. What makes you think the next time she comes on to you, you will be strong enough to resist?"

"She won't do that again. She promised. We're going to get married right away. She doesn't want to wait."

"Of course, she doesn't. She has an agenda, and you're at the center of it. You need to just stop, step back, and clear your head. The woman is on a mission, and there is no telling what she might do from day to day. Seducing you was a part of her plan, Dad, and, believe me, there is no way you can guarantee it won't happen again and again!"

"It won't, and you need to stop harassing me. I know what I'm doing."

"I beg to differ with you, Dad. No, you don't know what you are doing, and that scares me."

"When two people are in love—" Ben began.

"You're not in love, Dad. You're in lust! Lust! You've not only lost your senses, you're compromising your principles. You've entered into Satan's territory, Dad!"

Ben hung his head and seemed at a loss for words.

"You have to practice what you preach, Preacher! Sex outside the marriage bed is a sin," Forrest continued.

Ben thought for a moment. "All right, all right! I said it was a mistake. What do you want from me?"

Dr. Mildred Dumàs

"I want you to come to your senses. That's what I want."

"You don't understand, Son," Ben continued, his voice breaking.

My God, it's as if he's under some kind of spell," Forrest thought.

"Dad, do you really think the parishioners at your new church would approve of you marrying a woman like Ms. Cooper, or whatever her name might be? I'm sorry but she's just not First Lady material. You might lose a lot of members, and I can't say that I would blame them. You might even lose the church."

"I can't lose my church. Not after all that I've gone through to get it. I've, I've. . ." He stopped, looked up at his son, a confused look on his face.

"You're going to have to make a choice, Dad: the woman or the church. You can't have both. That just wouldn't work. The congregation of First St. Marks would not allow that to happen. Do you hear me?"

"They can't tell me what to do!"

"My God, Dad, can't you see what this is doing to you? Don't you know that marrying that woman would only make things worse?"

"You don't know anything about her?"

"And that's my point, Dad. Neither do you!"

"I know all I need to know! I know that I love her, and she loves me!"

"Stop deluding yourself!"

"So, you think it's impossible for her to love me? I'm not old and decrepit yet. I'm just sixty-seven."

"I'm not saying you're old and decrepit. I'm saying she's an indecent woman. Otherwise she wouldn't have been in your bed last night."

"Stop harping on that!"

"I'd love to stop harping on it, Dad, but I can't. You want to marry the woman, for God's sake! That just can't happen."

After a brief silence, Ben asked, "Will you marry us?"

Forrest looked at him aghast. "No, I will not marry you! Have you heard a word I've said? That would be against my better judgment. I'm a minister, and, unlike you, I have to be true to my convictions. I don't believe this woman would be a suitable wife for you! And believe me, neither will anyone else."

"That's not for you or others to say. I'm capable of making my own decisions!"

"I'm not so sure about that."

"Then I'll get somebody else." Ben got to his feet and left the table, his breakfast untouched.

"I went to see Mother McDonald yesterday," Forrest shouted to his father's retreating back.

Ben turned back around, a curious expression on his face. "Why did you do that?"

"To find out what's happening with you and those thugs from the church. I know everything, Dad."

"What did she tell you? Did she have one of her famous dreams?"

"She knows what's going on, Dad. God shows her things in her dreams."

Ben walked back over to the table and flopped back down into the seat he had just vacated. "That's what she says. All that hocus-pocus stuff. Now who's the fool?"

"I know they're threatening you. I know they're using the church as a bribe. Deacon Davis needed a puppet to help do his dirty work, and you're it, Dad."

"Stop it. You don't know what you're saying."

"You're ripping off your congregation. You're stealing from your members to help fund Davis' campaign."

Ben covered his face with his hands.

"They gave you an ultimatum, didn't they?"

Ben looked up at his son, an agonized look on his face. "I had to do it," he whispered.

Ben moved closer to his father. "No, you didn't. You don't have to do anything you don't want to do, Dad. We can walk away from all this corruption."

"I can't. It's gone too far."

"No, it hasn't, we--"

"Yes, it has! I signed an agreement."

"You what?"

"I agreed to it."

"Dad!" Forrest looked at his father, aghast.

"She said it was all right. She told me to do it."

"And that's another thing. How could you listen to that woman? Mother McDonald says she knew Ms. Cooper was trouble the day she walked into that church."

"You talked with her about Conswella?"

"I'm sorry, Dad. I, I mentioned to her that you said Ms. Cooper told you it was all right to ask for the twenty percent increase."

"Why are you telling other folk my business?"

"I'm just trying to help, Dad. This thing with Deacon Davis and his posse has gotten out of control. And you're the one who is really telling other folk your business. The things you are doing of late. The twenty percent increase in tithes, and now your decision to marry this, this wayward woman and make her the church's first lady. I don't have to say a word to anybody; you're doing a good job of exposing yourself on your own. If you don't believe me, just wait until you see the reaction of the members of First St. Marks if you make good on your threat to marry that woman."

"She's good for me, Son. We relate to each other. She's a good listener. She doesn't judge me like you do."

"Conswella? So that's it? She's dictating to you, too? You've been talking with that woman about this, and you can't talk to me, your own son?"

"We talked a little."

"I can't believe this! You go to a stranger with your problems, and you can't talk to your own son? My God! Am I blind or what? When did all this happen?"

"A few days ago. We went to lunch."

"You've been dating the woman? Going out in public with her?"

"It was just lunch. We started talking, and . . . She seemed really concerned about me. She told me she thought it was fair."

"The increase in tithes?" Forrest asked.

"Yes, she said the church is benefiting by having such an influential person as the mayor as a member. That it would all weigh out in the end. We went by Deacon Davis' office, and I signed the papers. I agreed to help."

"Help? Help Davis and his committee rip off your congregation? Did that really seem like the right thing to do, Dad? Did you stop to think about what you were doing before you did it?"

Ben got up from the table and started out of the room. "I'm going into town," he threw back over his shoulder.

"Are you going to see her?"

Ben stopped, whirled back around to face his son. "What if I am? Are you my judge and jury now? Who do you think you are?"

"I'll tell you who I am. I'm a minister; a member of the clergy; a man of God; a man of the cloth; a preacher of the gospel; a deliverer of the word; an ambassador of Christ; a personal witness of God's saving truth; a proclaimer of the gospel; a man with a message, a true message; a follower of Christ; a modern-day disciple—no Judas traits here, Dad! Can you say the same thing? Can you?"

Ben turned and hurried toward the door.

Forrest yelled after him. "You know about Judas, don't you, Dad? Do I need to tell you what Judas did?"

Ben went on out the door.

Forrest followed him. "Dad, are you going to see that woman?"

Forrest watched helplessly as his father fled the house. In a few moments, he heard the Mercedes roar to life and the garage door open.

Chapter Thirty-Eight

"We have to postpone the wedding." Forrest stood at the window in Sylvia's parent's living room. It was early evening. After his fight with his father that morning, he had gone to the church and worked with the secretary: getting out the bulletin for the next Sunday, designing tracts for Bible Study, and dictating correspondence.

His father had finally come into the office around noon. Forrest left. He was so upset about what his father was doing, he did not trust himself to keep quiet. He was afraid he and his father would begin arguing again right there in the church for others to see and hear. He was so ashamed, and did not know if he could control himself if the subject happened to come up there at the church.

He wasn't sure what might come out of his mouth.

He didn't want others to know how foolish his father was being about that woman. Planning to marry her . . . Good Lord! What would people think?

He didn't want to find out.

He had to find a way to stop his father from making a complete idiot of himself. What respect he had with this church would certainly diminish if he fulfilled his threat to marry Conswella Cooper.

He wanted to tell everyone who would listen about their new convert, Sister Cooper, but he knew he could not do that.

His and his father's livelihood was already being threatened. And maybe that would be a good thing. If they lost the church behind his father's stupidity, the house and all of the other amenities would be gone as well, so the blushing bride would probably disappear, because she would not get what she really wanted out of the deal. The title of First Lady of First St. Marks, the recognition and prestige that title would offer her, the elaborate lifestyle she would be living as the preacher's wife—in the mansion---would have been just a dream.

But surely everyone would see right through her charade—everyone except his father, the foolish old man lusting after a pretty young woman.

Then there was the money thing: Davis and his committee of thieves who were stealing from the church. He didn't know how much the office staff knew about what was going on at First St. Marks, and he didn't want to be the one to bring it to the forefront. Not yet, anyway. Or would he ever?

It was all just too much.

After a light lunch, Forrest went to the hospital to see some of their sick members. He had promised family members that he would do so, and he thought that was a perfect time. He could not go back to the office. That was for sure.

After he left the hospital, he went home. He was tired and needed some rest since sleep had completely eluded him the night before. He had literally tossed and turned all night trying to figure out what was happening to his father. He was tired of it all. He just wanted to be done with it. All of it. It wasn't worth the agony it was causing.

He wanted to just leave it all behind, and get on with his life.

Forrest looked at the clock on the nightstand beside his bed. It was four forty-five. Sylvia would be getting home from work in a few minutes. He had to see her.

~✷~

Forrest had been standing at the window in Sylvia's parents living room, looking out, seeing nothing for a few minutes, trying to think of a way to tell Sylvia that they had to postpone their wedding. He knew how disappointed she would be, but he had to do it. He had no choice.

She had sensed something was wrong. He could tell by the way she was looking at him. He decided to just blurt it out, just go ahead and tell her and suffer whatever consequences there might be. But he couldn't, in good conscience, go ahead with their plans to get married when his father needed him like he had never needed him before. *Even his life might be in danger*, Forrest thought. He could not desert him now. Not even to secure his future with the woman he loved.

"We have to postpone the wedding," he said softly.

"We can't, Forrest. We've made plans. We've. . ." Sylvia left the sentence dangling, her face aghast. "Are you breaking our engagement?"

"No," Forrest said, almost too quickly. "We just need to postpone it, just for a while."

"But why?"

"It's Dad."

She was beside him then. "What's wrong with your father? Is he sick?"

Forrest just looked at her for a moment.

"Is he all right?" Sylvia continued her voice anxious now.

"Yes. No. God, I don't know."

"You're not making sense, Forrest. Where is he? What's happened to your father?"

Forrest took her by the shoulders and backed her up against the sofa. She sat; he sat beside her. "He wants to get married."

"Married? To whom? I didn't even know he was seeing someone."

"God, I don't know how to tell you this." Forrest stood and started to walk away.

Sylvia grabbed his hand and pulled him back down onto the sofa. "Don't walk away from me, Forrest. Talk to me! Tell me what's going on!"

"That woman."

"What woman?"

"The woman I told you about. The woman in the red dress. Or she wore a red dress the first time she came to the church."

"The Cooper woman?"

"Yeah, the Cooper woman."

"He wants to marry her? Are you serious?"

"He is."

"But how . . .? He just met her, didn't he?"

"We both did. She has been coming on to him since the first day she came to church."

"That was fast. When did they start seeing each other?"

"I didn't know he had until last night." Forrest got up, walked back over to the window again. "I caught them. She was in his bed."

"Oh, my God. You mean they. . ." She left the sentence dangling.

"Oh, yeah, they sure did. I confronted her. She told me they were getting married."

Sylvia got up, walked over to him. "This is awful."

"You telling me?

"You've got to stop him. That would finish him as pastor of First St. Marks."

"I tried to tell him. He won't listen."

"How can he not listen? He's a minister. He knows what he's doing is wrong."

"He does."

"If what you told me about the woman is true, she sounds like a street walker, an opportunist. Can't he see that?"

Forrest just shook his head and looked blankly at her.

"Good, Lord, Forrest, it sounds as if the woman has him so mixed up, he—"

"It's as if he has lost his mind," Forrest said interrupting her.

"He'd be the laughing stock of the church—before they put him out, of course."

"I know. I know."

She looked at him, her eyes pleading. "So, we have to put our lives on hold because of this?"

"He's my father. I have to try to stop him from ruining his life."

"And in the meantime, you ruin our lives? The invitations have already been mailed and, and . . ." her voice broke.

He took her by the shoulders. "Sylvia, don't you understand what I'm going through here? Can't you see? I have to try to do something. I can't concentrate right now. I can't marry you while in this state of mind. What kind of husband do you think I would be with all this weighing on my mind? I can't drag you into this. It wouldn't be fair."

"How do I tell four hundred people we're not getting married?" Sylvia asked, tears flowing freely down her cheeks now.

"You don't. We are getting married. We just have to push the date."

"Everything has already been arranged."

He took her in his arms. "I'm sorry, baby."

She pulled away from him. "So am I."

"Sylvia . . . I have to do something."

She threw up a staying hand. "Don't. I don't know how to tell four hundred people not to come to our wedding. I don't know how to tell my parents. I don't know how to tell my minister. I don't know. . ." She was sobbing uncontrollably now. "I don't know how to not marry you." She turned and left him standing in the middle of her parent's living room looking lost and totally unnerved.

After a few moments, he let himself out the front door.

Dr. Mildred Dumàs

Chapter Thirty-Nine

"He's talking about marrying that woman," Forrest stood in Mother McDonald's living room. He had come back to see her. He had to talk with someone about what had happened and thought she would be the safest person in which to confide.

"I assume you mean Ms. Cooper."

"Yes, the Cooper woman!"

"That's bad. She's trouble."

"I know. I tried to tell him, but he won't listen."

"If she gets her clutches into him, there's no telling what might happen. I knew that woman was after something the day she came strolling up into that church. I just knew it, and I knew whatever she had on her mind was not a good thing. You have to convince your father that he could lose everything if he brings that woman up into that church as his wife. The members would not stand for it. Doesn't he know that?"

"No, he's oblivious. It's as if he has lost all sense of reality."

"He has to come to his senses before it's too late!"

"It might be too late. I, I caught them in bed together."

"Oh, my Lord," Mother McDonald exclaimed. "God help us! If he has taken up with that piece of trash, he has taken complete leave of his senses."

"Help me, Mother McDonald. What should I do?"

"You need to put him in that car and get away from this town as fast as you can."

Chapter Forty

Conswella pulled her silver Mercedes Benz off the highway onto the lookout point. The sun was just setting, and the view was magnificent. She had passed this area many times but had never stopped to really enjoy the view.

Today was no different. She was not there to enjoy the view.

The white Rolls Royce pulled into the parking space next to Conswella's Mercedes. Deacon Gaston Davis got out of the Rolls and walked over to the passenger side of the Mercedes.

Conswella rolled down the window and held out her hand.

Deacon Davis put a thick white envelope into Conswella's outstretched hand. "It's all there."

Conswella held the envelope in her hand, moving it up and down, as if weighing it. "I trust you." She smiled at him then put the envelope into her purse that sat beside her on the passenger seat.

"You'll get the rest after the ceremony."

Conswella smiled at him, rolled up the window, backed her car out of the parking space, turned it around, and pulled back onto the highway.

Chapter Forty-One

The flames were leaping all around her. The house was on fire. She had to get out, but how? Which way? She was surrounded by flames. They had spread so quickly. What had caused it? How had it happened?

Where was the door? Were there windows in the room? Yes, yes, there were windows, but which way? She had no idea. But she could not just stand there and burn to death. She had to get out. But there was no way out. The heat . . . it was so hot.

Then she felt the flames on her back and in her hair. She was burning to death. The smoke, it was strangling her.

She screamed, and the scream awakened her.

Mother McDonald jerked awake with a start. She looked about, trying to get her bearings. She was in her rocker in her upstairs bedroom. "It was a dream," she said, looking toward the heavens. "Oh, thank you, Jesus. Thank you. Thank you, Father."

She was so tired after eating her lunch. She had sat down to rest for a while and had fallen asleep. *Thank God it was only a dream; but it seemed so real,* she thought.

Her house had been on fire.

"Thank you, Lord," she said again.

She got up and moved over to the window. *Dusk, my favorite time of day,* she thought. She looked down on the street below. "Well, now," she said as she spotted a late model silver looking car driving slowly past her house. The driver looked up, and their eyes locked for a moment. The car sped away. "That was that woman. My God."

She went hurriedly to the telephone beside the bed, picked it up, and began to dial. A moment later, she spoke into the mouthpiece. "Sister, I need to get away for a while."

"What did you see?" her sister, Gwendolyn, asked from the other end of the line.

Mother McDonald chuckled. "You know me too well, my dear sister."

"Are you going to tell me?"

"I'm in a hurry. I have to pack."

"All right, you can tell me when you get here."

"I'll make my reservations and call you right back," Mother McDonald said.

Something was going on with that woman. What was the Cooper woman doing driving past her house? What business did she have in her neighborhood? Whatever the woman was doing, Mother McDonald knew it had something to do with her. Why else had she been looking up at her house? Why had she sped away when she saw her looking out of the window?

Her dream, the fire . . .? Could the woman possibly...? Would she even dare?

Maybe she was just being paranoid.

She would just leave for a few days and see.

It was dark now. Mother McDonald stood at her next-door neighbor's back door. A piece of luggage sat at her feet. She raised her hand and knocked. In a moment, her neighbor, Charlene Sullivan, mid-thirties, a bit on the plump side, with thick, cropped, brown hair framing a pretty round face, opened the door and squinted at her.

"Mother McDonald, what are you doing at the back door?" She flung the door wide, and spotted the piece of luggage. "Bill could have come over and gotten your luggage for you?"

"Oh, it's not that heavy. And I came to the back door, because I don't want all of our neighbors knowing I'm leaving town."

Charlene chuckled. "Good thinking. Come on in." She picked up the piece of luggage and set it just inside the door then stepped back to allow Mother McDonald to pass.

Mother McDonald stepped up into the room.

"We'll sneak you into the car through the kitchen door. You can lie down in the back seat when we drive out onto the street if you like," Charlene continued.

They chuckled.

"I'm almost ready. Bill's going to ride with us." Charlene closed the door.

"Great. It'll be good having him along. Then you won't have to drive back all by yourself. I hope I'm not inconveniencing you all too much."

"Not at all. Anytime you need us, just let us know."

"Thank you. Will the children be all right?"

"Of course, They're sleeping, and Tim is home. They'll be just fine. I hope your sister will be better soon."

"I'm sure she will."

"Just seeing you will probably make her feel better."

"I hope so."

Mother McDonald hated lying to her neighbors. They were good neighbors, good friends, and always ready to lend a helping hand. But what else could she do? She couldn't tell them that she had dreamed her house was on fire, and that somebody just might be planning to set it on fire and have them worrying about that and their house that was right next door, although the houses were a good distance apart. If what she expected were to happen, the fire department would surely be there before it

---

Dr. Mildred Dumàs

could spread to one side or the other. She prayed they would, if it actually happened, of course.

All she could do was wait and see.

"Is there anything else Bill and I can do for you?" Charlene asked.

"Just keep an eye on the house for me. It'll only be for a few days."

"We certainly will."

"And be careful," Mother McDonald said, her expression a bit pensive.

Chapter Forty-Two

Under the cover of darkness, the woman moved stealthily up the sidewalk toward the front door of the house. She carried a single key on a short blue ribbon in her right hand. She tried the key in the door. It did not work.

"Damn," she whispered.

She moved around to the side of the house and tried the key in the door there. She was in luck. The lock clicked. She opened the door and walked inside. *The back hallway,* she thought. She had been through every room, every nook and cranny of the place and remembered every detail. After all, it would be hers soon, her new home. She could not wait to become mistress of this grand manor. Oh, did she have plans for this place. If the members of First St. Marks thought it was the grandest place they had ever seen, just wait until she got through with the remodeling she had in mind.

Just wait.

All of this would certainly make up for having to marry the old fool in order to have it. And who said she had to continue this charade after the wedding, after her name had become Mrs. Benjamin Thomas. She had other plans. Yes, she did. And she knew just what to do to keep the old fool satisfied and his mouth shut.

It was late, so she knew the occupants of the house were probably sleeping. *Sleep tight, boys,* she thought. Then she smiled.

She stopped in the kitchen and hung the key on a hook beside the stove that sat next to the hallway.

Some people were such idiots. Who in his or her right mind would leave keys hanging beside an exit for anyone to pick up as they exited? That was one of the most foolish things anyone could do, that and putting keys under a mat at the front door.

Well, she guessed *foolish* was a good term to describe a lot of things that were going on in this town, and in this house. The foolish old man she was about to marry, for instance. Foolish was surely working for her. Yes, it was.

She chuckled, went through the dining room, then the living room and on up the stairs.

∾ঌৡৣৄ∾

What was happening? Wha . . .? *Am I dreaming again? I don't want this dream again, Lord. I, I* . . . Forrest's thoughts raced. He opened his eyes and tried to sit up. Something was holding him down. Something was on top of him. His mouth . . . he couldn't open his mouth. *Oh, my God. Oh, my God!* he thought.

He reached out and turned on the bedside lamp. She was astraddle him, kissing him hard on the lips, holding his face with her hands. He jerked his mouth away from hers.

"This is just the beginning," she whispered.

He rolled over and dumped her onto the floor. "Get off me, you filthy whore! What are you doing in my room? What are you doing in this house, in my bed?"

"You know you want me."

"Mother McDonald said you were trouble, but this . . . You pathetic piece of trash!"

Conswella jumped up from the floor, snatched her clothes from the foot of the bed, and raced from the room. He started after her then realized he did not have on any clothes. He always slept in the raw. He rushed to his closet, grabbed a robe, and put it on as he ran from the room.

The hallway was empty. He went on down the stairs.

He heard the car as it careened out of the back driveway.

He ran through the kitchen then down the back hallway. The back door was standing wide open. He closed and locked it, and then hurried back upstairs to his father's room. He began pounding on the locked door. "Dad! Dad!"

In a few seconds, Ben opened the door. "What's wrong?"

"She was here. She was in my room. She was in my bed."

"Who?"

"Conswella."

Ben tried to push the door shut; Forrest stuck his foot in it.

"You'd try anything to keep us apart, wouldn't you?" Ben snapped.

"Dad, I swear. She was in my room, in my bed. She was . . . she was trying to—"

"Oh, stop it, Forrest. Just stop it!" Ben said interrupting him.

"Dad, I'm telling you—"

Ben sneered at him. "Stop lying!" he said, interrupting Forrest again. "How did she get in the house? I locked up myself."

"I don't know, but she was here."

"You're lying!" Ben shouted.

He shoved his son. Forrest fell backwards into the hallway. Ben slammed the door shut and locked it.

Forrest jumped up and began pounding on his father's bedroom door with his fists. "Dad, open this door! We need to talk! You have to listen to me!"

"Get away from my door, do you hear me. Get away!"

"Dad," Forrest whispered, his head resting on the door.

After a moment he turned and ran back down the hallway to his room. He began yanking the bedclothes off the bed, throwing them in a heap on the floor.

"Nasty!" he screamed. "Everything about her is nasty! Everything she does is nasty!"

He picked up the bedclothes from the floor and raced down the hallway to the stairs. He bounded down them, and ran on through the house to the back hallway. He opened the back door, ran outside and on over to the waste can.

He opened the can and dumped the bedclothes inside, slammed the top back onto the can, and then just stood there breathing hard, his mind racing.

He looked toward the heavens and screamed. "God, help me! Help me!"

Chapter Forty-Three

The silver Mercedes drove slowly past the house. It was late, and the neighborhood looked so peaceful. "Not a thing is stirring. Not even a mouse," the driver said to herself.

She smiled.

She went on around the block then drove slowly back to the house. She stopped in front of it and looked up at the second floor. "The old bat's probably sound asleep," Conswella said to herself. *The bedrooms are probably up there. Well, sleep tight, you old hag. Sweet dreams. This will be your last trip to dreamland, so have a good one,* she thought. She drove on past the house. "One, two, three, four," she counted the houses aloud as she passed them. *Far enough,* she thought. She stopped the car and backed into a parking spot in front of the fifth house down the block.

She got out of the car and closed the door softly. She did not pop the trunk; instead, she opened it with her key and raised the lid ever so gently. She picked up a pair of gloves from a small box inside the trunk and put them on her hands. Then she removed a pair of rubber boots from the trunk and put them on her feet. She then took two one-gallon cans from the trunk and set them gently on the sidewalk. She brought the trunk lid down and pushed it quietly into place. She picked up the two cans and tiptoed back down the sidewalk to her target. She went around the right side of the house where she set one of the cans on the ground. She then went on to the back of the house with the other can. She set the can down then bent down and unscrewed the cap. She began to pour liquid from the can all around the back of the house and around the left side. She came back to the right side of the house, opened the second can, and poured the liquid around that side of the house, doubling back around back until the can was empty. "This will teach you to meddle in my business, old woman," she whispered to herself.

When both cans were empty, she gathered them, walked back to the car, and put them in the trunk. She came back to the house, went around to the back, stood a few feet away, pulled a book of matches out of her pocket, struck one, and threw it toward the house. Flames instantly shot up engulfing the back of the house and snaking around the sides. She hurried back around the side of the house and down the sidewalk to her car. She got in, quietly closed the door, and then drove off down the street.

Little Jerome was thirsty. He always got thirsty at night. He got out of bed and crept down the hallway, careful not to awaken his mother and father—and certainly not his big brother. Tim was mean to him sometimes.

He tiptoed past Tim's door and went on into the kitchen. He turned on the light, pulled the stepstool over to the sink, and climbed up onto it. He got a glass from the cabinet beside the sink and was about to climb down when he squinted, looking toward the window. There was something moving outside the window. He got down off the stool, walked back over to the door, and turned out the light. He went back to the stool, got back up onto it, and pulled back the curtains at the window.

He jumped off the stool and raced into his parents' room. "Daddy, Mommy!"

Chapter Forty-Four

"I'm sorry about last night, Son. I didn't mean to push you like that. I don't know what possessed me to do such a thing." Ben looked down the long table at his son who sat at his usual spot at the other end.

Both of them picked at their food.

Forrest had cooked again. The food was passable, he guessed, but even he did not feel much like eating this morning. His mind was too full of the events that had occurred the night before. In fact, the apology his father had just made to him told him that they were both consumed with the same thoughts.

What was that woman trying to do? She wanted to marry his father, so she could become First Lady of the church, have a home—a lavish home, have access to a new car, have money to spend as she wished, and she wanted him on the side? Was she crazy, or what? He had heard of situations like this: the father's young wife and the son or stepson having an affair.

Well, she was grossly mistaken if she thought she could have him. He would not be an accessory to her ploy to nab his father and all that he was worth right then.

He had to find a way to get the woman out of their lives before she accomplished her goal of marrying his father. He had to do so. He had no choice. The woman would ruin everything for him and his father. *If the church found out what happened here at the mansion . . .* he thought. If his father continued with his plan to marry the woman . . .

His father was completely out of control. What if she was feeding him something that could alter his personality? What if—

"I'm so sorry, Son. Please forgive me." Ben said interrupting Forrest's thoughts.

"I forgive you, Dad."

His father had never laid a hand on him in anger—certainly not since he had been a grown man. That had been a first, and he just did not know what to think of it.

"Things have gotten so out of hand, Dad. But what I said was true. The woman was in my room, in my bed."

"It was a dream."

"No, Dad, it was no dream."

"But I locked up myself. There was no way she could have gotten into the house. And if you're thinking I let her in, you're wrong. I didn't."

Forrest thought for a moment. "Mrs. Barber's key . . . Did she give it to you?"

Ben dropped his head. "No, she didn't say a word to me."

I guess not. She was too embarrassed watching you carrying on with that woman, Forrest thought. "I don't remember seeing it," he said. He got up and hurried into the kitchen. He pulled the key with the blue ribbon from the hook beside the stove and looked at it curiously. "Has it been there all this time?" he whispered.

He went back into the dining room, dangling the key for his father to see. "It was on the hook where she always put it, but I don't remember seeing it there earlier today. Who all has keys to this house, Dad?"

"Just us and Deacon Davis."

"Are you sure?"

"That's what he told me."

"Well, I'm going to make sure. I'm going to change the locks."

"You can't do that." Ben gave his son a fearful look. "This is the church's house."

My God, he's afraid to do anything that he thinks would upset those men, Forrest thought. His father was not usually a gullible man, but those people were getting to him in a way Forrest could not have ever imagined. He was changing right before his eyes, and there did not seem to be a thing he could do about it. But he was darn sure going to try. "Dad, this is our home while we're living here, and we have to do all we can to make sure we are safe here," he said.

"But they have to have a key."

"Why?"

"I don't know. It's the rule."

"Well, I'm breaking that rule."

"You can't!"

"I am." Forrest got up and walked over to his father, who looked up at him fearfully. "You let me handle this. Everything's going to be all right."

"I, I don't know, Son."

"I can handle this, Dad, but if you marry that woman—"

"You just can't let it alone, can you?" Ben said interrupting him. "Stop trying to tell me what I can and cannot do! And stop lying about my fiancée."

"I'm not lying, Dad. What I said about last night was true. It was not a dream!"

"Stop saying that, Son. She's my fiancée. She loves me, and I love her. She wouldn't do such a thing. She's—"

"She's a slut, dad." Forrest said interrupting him. "She is a nasty, filthy, gold-digging, piece of trash!"

Ben leapt to his feet, his chair banging the floor behind him. "I don't have to sit here and listen to you berate the woman I'm going to marry. I'm going to get ready for church." He started swiftly from the room.

Forrest followed him. "She was in my bed, on top of me, kissing me, fondling me! I woke up to your fiancée trying to have sex with me, the son of the man she has promised to marry, the man to whom she has pledged her undying love, the man she's trying to lure into her web, so she can use him!"

"Liar!" his father shouted, not breaking his stride as he started up the stairs.

"If I'm lying, may God strike me dead right now!"

Ben stopped and turned around to face his son. He looked at Forrest for a moment, a flicker of doubt on his face, and then he turned and went on up the stairs, leaving his son looking after him until he crested the stairs and disappeared from sight.

Forrest's cell phone rang. He picked it up from the table beside his plate of uneaten food. Now his and his father's dire situation was interfering with his appetite as well. "Hello," he said into the phone. After a moment, he continued. "Oh, my God! Is she all right?" Another moment passed then he spoke again. "I'll be right there." He put his phone into his pocket, grabbed his keys from the table, and picked up his briefcase from the floor beside his chair.

I have to tell Dad, he thought, and then instantly thought better of the idea. In the state his father had been of late, he didn't think *the pastor* of First St. Marks would be of any help in this new situation that was threatening one of his members.

Forrest hurried through the house to the garage. He got into their old Cadillac, backed it hurriedly out of the garage, and sped off down the street.

Chapter Forty-Five

Forrest and one of the men from the church, Deacon Richard Stanton, stood in front of Mother McDonald's house.

"It's not bad, but as you can see, smoke is still rising," said Stanton.

"How did it happen?" Forrest asked.

They spoke without looking at each other, their eyes still on the smoldering fire.

"They know an accelerant was used, so they know someone started it." Deacon Stanton said. "The back received most of the damage, so it must have started back there. The sides are seared. The inside of the house is a little smoky, but no real damage."

"When did you get here?"

"A little over an hour ago. The neighbors called me right after the fire department left. Their little boy got up in the middle of the night and went to the kitchen to get a drink of water. He saw the flames out of the kitchen window there." Deacon Stanton pointed to the house next door.

"Did you talk with the boy?"

"Talked with all of them. That boy's thirst saved Mother McDonald's house. God sure does work in mysterious ways."

"Yes, he does," Forrest agreed.

"Thank God she was away."

"When did she leave?"

"Last night, I called her this morning after I got here. She'll be back Tuesday."

They were quiet for a moment then Deacon Stanton spoke again. "I called you, because she told me you had been to see her."

"Yes, we have been talking. What's going on, Deacon Stanton? Why aren't you involved in all of the secret meetings with Davis and the others?"

"Ah, that's some ungodly stuff that's going on, Reverend Thomas, and I want no part of it. Did she tell you?"

"Yes."

"We've been friends for a long time. She has no family. I'm her contact person whenever she needs help."

"That's good to know."

"And we talk a lot about a lot of things."

"The congregation needs to know what's going on, Deacon Stanton."

"I agree. They will in due time. Those people are dangerous."

"How did all this begin?"

"It's a long story."

"Have you had breakfast?" Forrest asked.

"No."

Chapter Forty-Six

"It all started the year Davis joined the church. I believe he came in with an agenda," Stanton said.

Deacon Stanton and Forrest sat in a booth at Grandma Mary's Downhome Cafe having breakfast. Their conversation was strained. Although Forrest knew what Stanton was telling him about Davis and his army of demons was true, he still had a hard time digesting it. But, then, Stanton was confirming what Forrest had been thinking all along, that Davis and his cronies were evil incarnate.

"In less than six months, he had gone through deacon's training and gotten himself on the Deacon Board. In less than a year, he was chairman of that board. How he did that, nobody knows. Or if they do, they are not telling. Deacon Reed who was chairman at the time simply disappeared about two weeks after Davis took his place."

"Disappeared? The man just vanished with no word to anybody?" Forrest asked.

"That's about it," Stanton said. "No one ever heard from him again. We think he was paid to do the disappearing act."

"Paid off, paid to disappear. I just hope his disappearance wasn't permanent, that he's still alive."

"Mother McDonald assured us that he was alive and well. She saw money changing hands."

"In one of her dreams?"

"So, you know about the dreams?"

"Yes, she told my father and me that the Lord shows her things in her dreams sometimes. My father thinks it's all some kind of hocus-pocus"

"And what do you think?"

"I believe her."

Deacon Stanton nodded his head in agreement. "Your father needs to listen to her." He paused for a moment then continued. "I think the good Lord gave Mother McDonald that gift, and she uses it wisely. She has helped so many people around the church."

"I heard about some of the things she has done."

Stanton smiled. "All good things. She hasn't been wrong about any of her predictions yet. Not one." He paused a moment then continued. "I heard about your father and the woman."

"Conswella . . . Have the rumors spread so soon?"

"Not yet. Just Davis, his crew, a few others, and I know at this point. Davis has a whistleblower in his camp who reports to me and I report to a few other people."

"How did you get so special?" Forrest asked.

"Somebody has to stay on top of things."

"If you know what's going on, why haven't you put a stop to it?

"It's not that easy. Things take time. We think we might have to go beyond our local police department. The chief and Davis are buddies, have been for years. The chief thinks our illustrious mayor can do no wrong, or maybe the chief is also on Davis' payroll. Now wouldn't that be something?"

"That's a shame," Forrest said.

"Yes, it is, but things are looking up. The whistleblower decided he wanted to become a whistleblower just about seven months ago. He got tired of being a part of all the corruption, the stealing, other crimes, and maybe even murder. But he decided, probably for his own good, that he could do more if he stayed on the inside."

"He might be right," Forrest offered. "You know I've been meaning to check up on our newest member, Ms. Cooper. I want to see what I can find out about her."

"No need. She's a plant, a prostitute Davis picked up in Vegas."

"I knew it! I knew she was nothing but a hooker. My God, what has my father gotten himself into?"

"She's on the payroll. Davis hired her to seduce your father, to pull him into his web. We don't know how far he plans to take it yet."

"Marriage. My father is talking about marrying the woman."

"Good, Lord! Marriage? He wants your father to marry the woman?"

"And my father is so ready and willing."

"Davis must have something big in mind."

"And my father is at the center of it. When will his reign of terror end?" Forrest asked.

"When somebody stops him. He has been doing this for so long, he has gotten comfortable with it, and because he has been allowed to continue for so long without being stopped, he must think he's invincible about now. I guess somebody—and I guess that somebody might have to be me—has to prove him wrong," said Stanton.

"Please! My father's life might depend on it."

"Is it that bad?"

"He's a totally different person, and it's getting worse every day."

"I understand Davis paid your ex-housekeeper to keep her mouth shut about the, the . . ."

"The seduction of my father, a middle-aged man, by that young woman, whoever she is," Forrest said, finishing the sentence for Stanton. "That's what it was, plain and simple, a seduction. Just think what will happen when people find out about it: the new minister and the prostitute. I tried to tell him."

"I guess we all have to find our own way," said Stanton.

"So, he paid her off with some of the church's money?" Forrest said.

"You got it. He's in that treasury as if it belongs to him." Stanton chuckled. "Yes, he paid her off, but just how long can a person sit on something as hot as this? Only God knows."

"How corrupt can one person be? We often say that there is some good in everybody. Maybe that doesn't apply to a man like Davis," Forrest offered.

"Deacon Reed was a good man. A good Christian man, so I just don't understand how he could have allowed himself to be . . ." Stanton left the sentence dangling, his voice trailing off.

"Money. It can make people—even the best of us—do all sorts of things sometimes."

"True. True."

"So, Davis paid Reed to disappear?"

Deacon nodded. "That's what we assumed."

"With the church's money."

"With the church's money."

"Tell me about Pastor Simms and the alleged murder and suicide."

"That's another thing. We don't' think it was a murder and a suicide; we believe it was murder, plain and simple."

"You think Davis . . .?"

"I wouldn't put it past the man."

"He has to be stopped."

"I know."

"My father was resisting."

"I heard." Stanton paused a moment. "But they wore him down."

"I could see it coming. I tried to prevent it, Deacon Stanton." Forrest's voice broke. "I tried."

"Maybe there is still hope," Stanton offered.

What? What can I do? I can't get him to listen."

Deacon Stanton looked Forrest straight in the eyes and said, "Run."

Chapter Forty-Seven

"God does work in mysterious ways." Ben stood at the pulpit. His face was somber. "I understand Mother McDonald's house caught on fire last night. Thank God she was out of town."

There were exclamations from many of the parishioners who had not heard about the fire. *Out of town*, Conswella thought. She sat on the end of the second row of seats on the left side of the church. She wore a sky-blue dress, not too short now—she had to begin looking and acting more like a real church lady if she was going to be the first lady of this place—and matching shoes. One of those shoes was on a foot that was attached to a perfectly shaped, nylon draped, leg that swung as far out into the aisle as its owner could manage.

She really liked to sit on the front row, but the deacons and the trustees occupied the first two rows in the middle section; the mothers occupied the first row on the right side; and the deaconesses sat on the front row on the left. She didn't know how she had found a front-row seat the first Sunday she had come, but she had, and she had scored—big time.

The leg stopped its swinging. Conswella sat straight up in her seat; the once swinging foot came to rest on the floor in front of her. *The old bitch was not home?* she thought.

"Yes, the Lord will guide us. If we just listen and trust in Him." Ben continued.

Conswella rose. She had to get out of that church so she could think. This was going to slow everything down between her and the preacher man. That nosy, old heifer had gotten away. Conswella knew the woman was not going to stop. Somebody had to stop her.

She would not fail again.

She went on out the door, got into her car, and sped away from the church. She would think of some lie to tell her fiancé when she saw him later.

Where is she going? Ben thought when he saw Conswella leaving the church. What had happened? He had to . . .

He heard Forrest clear his throat behind him, and realized that he had stopped speaking. How long had he been just standing there watching after Conswella? What had he been saying?

"Please turn your Bibles to . . ."

Forrest was so ashamed of his father and the way he was carrying on with that woman. He couldn't even concentrate on his sermon for watching the woman as she walked out of the church. He wondered when the church members were going to find out about their pastor and the prostitute. He had told Ben what Deacon Stanton said about the woman being a hired hooker, but Ben refused to believe it.

Dr. Mildred Dumàs

Chapter Forty-Eight

Deacon Davis got into his car. He was livid. In a moment his car sped out of the church parking lot. "The stupid cunt!" he yelled to himself.

Fifteen minutes later he stood outside the Claridge Apartment Building. He punched a series of buttons on a keypad at the front entrance. In a moment, a female voice asked, "Who is it?"

"Davis. Open the damn door!" he said.

The door clicked.

He entered the lobby then hurried to an elevator, stepped inside and punched the up button. In a few moments, he stepped out onto the fifth floor, and hurried to Apartment number 550. He rang the doorbell.

Conswella opened the door. Davis hurried inside, slamming the door behind him. "You did it didn't you?"

"What?" Conswella asked.

"Don't play the fool with me. You know exactly what I'm talking about. You stupid cunt! Who told you to try to burn down the old woman's house—with her in it for God's sake?"

"She was getting in my way."

He slapped her, sending her stumbling back across the floor. The back of her legs hit the sofa, and she fell onto it. A trembling hand went to the side of her face where he had hit her.

She looked up at him, her eyes blazing. "If you ever hit me again, I'll kill you," she said, her voice so soft it was barely audible. But he could see that she meant what she said. A glint of fear registered in his eyes, but only for a moment.

"You do nothing unless it's an order from me. Do you understand me? The woman is running her mouth about strange things happening around the church, about her damn dreams. Who knows what all she's saying, who she's saying it to, and about whom she's talking."

Conswella just glared at him, breathing heavily, her breasts rising and falling. She was beyond angry. *I want to see you dead, you slimy bastard."* she thought.

"Do you understand me?" he cut into her thoughts.

"Yeah, Davis, I understand."

"And that old fool. You just couldn't wait, could you? You just had to show him what you can do in bed, didn't you?"

"His son was preaching to him, and that old woman was telling him what to do. They might have gotten through to him if I hadn't taken things into my own hands. Now you can bet I'll be the only thing on his mind from his waking hour until he falls asleep at night—and then I'm going to be in his dreams. I know my job. You just stay in your lane and keep the hell out of mine!"

"You're supposed to be a Christian woman now. A Christian woman would not have jumped in the man's bed so soon."

"You told me to reel him in. Well that's about the best way I know to get a man to do anything you want."

"I don't know how your pimp handled you, but I call the shots here. Do you understand?

She just looked at him.

"Do you understand?" he repeated.

"Yeah," she said.

Dr. Mildred Dumàs

"Wait for my orders! "I have to make a few calls to clean up your latest mess! Go on in the bedroom and get ready for me," he snapped.

She glared angrily at him for a moment then walked out of the room.

Davis pulled his cell phone from his pocket and began to dial. In a moment he spoke into the phone. "Get the men and go over to Mother McDonald's house. Now!" He listened for a moment. "I know she's out of town. Go anyway. Let her neighbors know that First St. Marks takes care of its members, especially its elderly. Go next door and speak with the little boy that saw the fire. Praise him. Let him know what a good citizen he is. Make a good showing. We'll meet tomorrow morning as planned."

Davis put his phone back in his pocket, strolled into Conswella's bedroom, and shut the door behind him.

Chapter Forty-Nine

"He's not being faithful to you, you know," Deacon Stanton said.

"I know," Octavia Davis said.

They sat across from each other in *Preston's*, an upscale restaurant some twenty miles east of Clarksville. This was their favorite meeting place away from the city, away from the prying eyes of the parishioners of First St. Marks Baptist Church.

This was their hide-away.

"He's with her now," Stanton pressed on.

"I don't want to hear it, Richard."

"I want to be with you. Come home with me. Stay with me tonight."

"You know I can't do that. I'm a married woman, and we just don't do that."

"He's not worthy of you. Divorce him, and marry me."

Octavia smiled at him. "I made a vow before God."

"The vows have been broken many times by him," Stanton countered.

"He'll have to answer for that. That's between him and God."

"You don't deserve this."

"I know."

"I love you."

"I know." She reached across the table and took his hand. "It's your love that keeps me sane."

Their eyes met, his pleading, hers glistening with tears.

Chapter Fifty

Mother McDonald returned home that Tuesday as she said she would. "Praise the Lord," she said when she saw that her house was still standing and that her neighbors' houses on both sides of her were not harmed.

Deacon Stanton was standing outside the house waiting for her when her taxi pulled up to the curb. He hurried over, opened the back door, and helped her out of the car.

"Hello, Mother. Welcome home," He said, kissing her on the cheek.

"Thank you, Deacon Stanton. I see it's still standing. Thank the Lord."

"Thank the Lord," He repeated.

The taxi driver brought her piece of luggage around to the side of the car where they were standing. Deacon Stanton pulled out his wallet.

"How much?" he asked the driver.

"Oh, no, I can pay," Mother McDonald protested.

"Not today," Deacon Stanton said.

The driver told him the fare, he paid, and then the driver got back into the car and drove off down the street.

"Thank you."

"My pleasure. Where do you want to start?"

"Where did the fire start?"

"In the back."

"Then why don't we start there?"

"All right." Stanton picked up her piece of luggage, took it up on the porch, and set it down by the front door.

He came back down the steps, took Mother McDonald by the arm, and led her to the back of her house. "An accelerant was used. Somebody started it," Stanton said.

"I know," she said.

"You saw it. You know who did it?"

"No, I didn't *see* who did it, but I saw the fire. However, I did see someone surveying the area earlier that evening, and I thought it was rather strange. That's why I left town."

He stopped and looked at her curiously. "Who?"

"The Cooper woman," she said.

"Good, Lord!" he said.

<hr />

They had been in the house only a few minutes when the doorbell rang. "I'll get it," Stanton said. He went to answer the door.

Sister McDonald continued wiping down the kitchen walls. The place smelled of smoke, and some had seeped into the house somehow.

Stanton came back into the kitchen with the whole First St. Marks Mothers' Board in tow. They stood just inside the kitchen door with buckets, pails, sponges, cleansers, rubber gloves, air freshener, mops, dusters, and smiles on their faces.

"Where do we start?" asked Mother Moore.

Mother McDonald laughed, and then walked over and hugged every one of them.

"I'll call the insurance company," Stanton said and disappeared into other parts of the house.

A few minutes later, the house was buzzing with conversation, laughter, and busy ladies scrubbing walls, sweeping and mopping floors, dusting, cleaning windows, and anything else that looked like it could use a good swipe or two.

When the doorbell rang again, Stanton eagerly went to answer it. He was having a hard time trying to stay out of the way of the ladies. He opened the door, and there stood Deacon Davis, some of the other deacons, and a few of the trusties.

"Gentlemen," Stanton, said. He stood back and allowed the men to enter the house. "It's so good of you to come."

"This is what we do," said Davis.

"Yeah," Stanton said. *I know all about what you do, he thought.*

The men ended up outside, cleaning up the debris around the sides of the house, while the ladies continued cleaning on the inside. The delicious smell of food cooking was wafting throughout the house. After a hard day's work, everybody was sure to be hungry. That was a given.

Mother McDonald was not delighted with the presence of some of her guests that day, but she was always cordial to anyone who crossed her doorsteps. She knew why they had come. The deceivers, the pretenders.

She smiled. She had something for them. Yes, she did.

In the meantime, as soon as her last guest left, she was going to see little Jerome. Deacon Stanton had told her what her littlest neighbor had done. She had brought him a souvenir, and she wanted to give him a big kiss.

Praise God for the children, she thought.

Dr. Mildred Dumàs

Chapter Fifty-One

"I haven't seen you in two weeks!" Sylvia snapped.

"I called," Forest said.

They sat on the sofa in her parent's living room. She had called him earlier that afternoon and told him she needed to see him. He hated to leave his father at the house by himself, but she was his fiancée, and he did owe her an explanation. It had been a while since he had seen her. Two weeks? He hadn't realized. His father needed him. He was--

"Sure, you've called. Maybe three times," her voice cut into his thoughts.

"I'm trying, Sylvia. My father—"

"I'm so tired of hearing about your father. Why don't you just let him live his life and you live yours? We're supposed to be engaged."

"We are engaged. I love you."

"Then when are we going to get married?" We canceled our plans once because of your father, but we never made other ones. What am I supposed to think, Forrest? What am I supposed to do while you babysit your father?"

"You don't understand."

"No, I guess I don't." Sylvia removed the engagement ring from her finger, picked up his hand, put the ring in it, and closed his fingers around it.

She got up, walked to the front door, and opened it. She stood back waiting for him to leave.

"Sylvia, I—" he began.

"I can't do this anymore, Forrest," she said interrupting him.

"Sylvia, don't do this."

"Please leave."

He got to his feet, opened his hand, looked at the ring for a second, then put it in his pocket. He walked to the door, stopped for a moment, looking at her, then turned and walked out the door.

She slammed it behind him.

Chapter Fifty-Two

It was a bright Saturday morning, and one of the postmen in Clarksville, Preston Weaver, had several boxes filled with what seemed to be an anonymous letter to deliver. Just the addressees' names and addresses and a single stamp were on the front of the envelope. There was no return address.

Preston made it his business to get to know all of the people on his route—even a few families that had moved in during the past few months. It was good for business and netted him nice bonuses at Christmas time.

He also knew a lot about the personal lives of the people on his route.

All of those anonymous letters seemed to be going to members of the prestigious First St. Marks Baptist Church. Preston loved the mothers from First St. Marks. In the winter, they gave him hot chocolate and coffee; in the summer, they met him at the door with iced tea or lemonade to take along on his route.

What was going on now? *Not another scandal*, he thought. That church had had enough of those to last a lifetime. It wasn't tax season, so it couldn't be the members' donation documents.

So, what in the world could it be?

Other postmen and postwoman about town, and in surrounding cities, had the same issue as Preston.

The first anonymous letter Preston delivered was to Mother Moore. She saw him coming and met him at the door.

"Good morning, Preston. How are you doing today?" she said.

"I'm just fine, Mother Moore. How are you?

She chuckled. "Blessed and highly favored."

He laughed. He loved hearing the saints give him all of those old religious greetings. "So am I, Mother Moore. So am I." He handed her an electric bill, a telephone bill, and the anonymous letter.

"Would you like to come in for coffee?" she asked.

"I'd love to, Mother Moore, but I'm running a little late today. May I get a rain check?"

"Anytime," she said.

He wanted to ask her to read the letter while both of them drank a cup of her freshly brewed coffee, but of course, he could not do that even if he had had time for coffee. He had had a long night that put him in bed a few hours past his bedtime. He would have to watch his nights out with the boys.

He would just keep his ears to the ground. He would surely hear something soon. Not much went on in the town of Clarksville that Preston Weaver did not know about sooner or later.

Yes, other postmen and postwomen about town, and in surrounding cities, had the same issue as Preston. They all knew it was going to be a long day.

Mother Moore went into her kitchen, laid her mail on the table, and poured herself a cup of her freshly brewed—in her coffee pot, not in that thing, that Keurig thingamajig that everybody was so crazy about nowadays--Columbian coffee. She then poured a generous amount of her favorite creamer and a teaspoon and a half of raw honey into her freshly brewed

Dr. Mildred Dumàs

coffee. She took a sip and smiled. *Just right,* she thought. She sat down at her table to enjoy.

She opened her electric bill first, looked at the amount that she owed and smiled. Thank God it's autumn," she said to herself. The weather was just right. She didn't need the heat or the air conditioning. She took another sip of her coffee.

She opened her telephone bill next. It was still the same. "Thank God for those nice people," she said to herself. The telephone company had a program for low income people and she qualified. Now that was a real blessing. She took another sip of her coffee.

Mother Moore then opened her last piece of mail: the letter with no return address on it. "Now who could this be from?" she asked herself. She slid the letter from the envelope and began to read. Her eyes grew wide, and then her mouth fell open. She began to read faster. When she finished reading the letter, she could not believe what she had just read, so she read the whole thing again.

Her good, freshly-brewed coffee was forgotten.

Mother Moore leapt up from the table and moved over to the end of the counter where her telephone sat. She picked up the receiver and began to dial, but then remembered that the letter had said not to share any of the contents with anyone until First St. Marks' Church Meeting the next Saturday.

She put the phone back into its cradle, went into her family room and sat in her rocking chair. She began to rock.

The rocker was her favorite place for thinking, and did she have some thinking to do this day.

Chapter Fifty-Three

The next Saturday, at nine o'clock in the morning, the members of the First St. Marks Baptist Church gathered for the *Meeting of the Saints of First St. Marks Baptist Church*. In other words, the members of First St. Marks Baptist Church gathered for the church's quarterly meeting.

These meetings were always held in the sanctuary, because that was the only place that was large enough to hold all of the members. Usually only approximately three fourths of the members of First St. Marks came to these meetings. However, for some reason, this meeting packed the house.

Microphones were set up in the aisles, as usual, for those wanting to express their opinions or ask questions about various matters.

They sang a song, the deacons prayed, the secretary read the minutes from the last quarterly meeting, old business was rehashed, new business was introduced, and then things heated up a bit.

Mrs. Minnie Rockford hurried to one of the microphones. She held up the anonymous letter she had received in the mail. "Pastor Ben, I have a letter here that I would like to read to the members here today—just in case some of them did not receive—"

"No, that will not be allowed. You are out of order, Mrs. Rockford. Please sit down!" Deacon Gaston Davis yelled into a nearby microphone interrupting Mrs. Rockford.

There was a rustling in the auditorium as the church members pulled their letters out of pockets, purses, etc.

"I will not sit down, Deacon Davis. I have a right—"

"My wife has something to say, Deacon Davis, and I suggest you let her say it." This came from the husband of Mrs. Minnie Rockford, Joe Ben Rockford, retired heavyweight boxer, who had joined his wife at the microphone.

"And I suggest you and your wife take your seats, Mr. Rockford!" Davis shot back.

Rockford sometimes saw fit to come out of retirement whenever he encountered a situation that he thought warranted his attention. Apparently, this was one of those situations.

It happened so fast no one could believe it.

Rockford was upon Davis before the guards standing around the walls even realized what was about to happen.

Rockford, better known as *the Black Rock* crashed into Davis knocking him back into several other deacons that stood behind him. It took four guards to quiet down Rockford and get him back to his seat, and all ten of them to help bring order back to the gathered assemblage that was now in an uproar.

"You need to take charge here," Forrest said to his father.

Ben looked at his son blankly for a moment, and then began to blabber. "I, I can't. I don't know what to do. I, I . . . ."

"Well, I do," Forrest said. He got up, went to the pulpit, and spoke into the microphone. "Please take your seats everyone! Take your seats everyone, please—except for Sister Rockford. My father is not feeling well right now, so as your assistant pastor I shall be conducting the rest of this meeting."

Everyone took their seats as their assistant pastor had asked them to do.

I'm going to sue that bastard for all he's worth and then some. And just wait until I get my hands on whoever wrote that letter, Davis thought as he and the two men who had broken his fall went back to their seats.

When the assemblage was quiet again, Forrest gestured toward Mrs. Rockford. "Please read the letter," Sister Rockford.

Mrs. Rockford smiled at Forrest. "Thank you, Pastor Forrest."

She began to read.

"'My dear sisters and brothers of First St. Marks Baptist Church. I am about to share with you something most of you will not believe. Some of you might have heard what I am about to tell you before; most of you probably have not. But after today, none of you can say you did not know. I recently learned, by listening to preachers on the internet, that God wants us to stop tithing.'"

There were gasps, exclamations, and rustling sounds throughout the auditorium.

"'That's right. You heard me correctly. That's what those preachers are saying, that the Bible tells us we are not under the laws of the Old Testament anymore. We are under grace now, and we should learn grace and start giving. Giving because we want to give, not because we are forced, or commanded to do so. Tithing is not giving; it is a mandate, and God wants us to be givers. Second Corinthians 9:7.'"

"'*Every man according as he purposeth in his heart, so let him give; not grudgingly, or of necessity; for God loveth a cheerful giver.*'" Forrest interjected. "Read on, Sister Rockford."

Sister Rockford reads.

"'The preachers said that there is no commandment in the new testament that says Christians must tithe. Tithing is weak and beggarly. Galatians 4:9.'"

Forrest quotes from the Bible. "'*But now, after that ye have known God, or rather are known of God, how turn ye again to the weak and beggarly elements, whereunto ye desire again to be in bondage?*'" He gives Sister Rockford a nod.

Sister Rockford continues.

"'The preachers admitted that some ministers encourage their members to tithe for personal gain, to put money in their own pockets, to set themselves up in mansions, behind the wheels of fancy cars, and even in air planes. Not to give to the poor, the widows, or for the building of God's kingdom. Not for missionary work, not for saving souls. They encourage their members to give so they can get. That's dirty money, money gained by lying and deception. Taking is not giving; it is a mandate. So, don't listen to the gainsayers.'"

Forrest interjects. "'*Holding fast the faithful word as he hath been taught, that he may be able by sound doctrine both to exhort and to convince the gainsayers. For there are many unruly and vain talkers and deceivers . . . whose mouths must be stopped.* Titus, chapter one, verses nine through eleven,'" He beckoned for Mrs. Rockford to continue.

She reads again.

"'We should give because we are thankful. First Thessalonians 5:18'"

Forrest interjects again. "'*In everything give thanks, for this is the will of God in Christ Jesus concerning you.*'" He gestures for Mrs. Rockford to continue.

She does.

"'God will not curse you if you don't tithe as preachers like to point out in Malachi 3:9.'"

Forrest interjects again. "'*Ye are cursed with a curse: for ye have robbed me, even this whole nation.*'" He nods to Mrs. Rockford.

She continues reading.

"'The preachers said that is nothing but a guilt trip, and a lot of preachers use it to make their members feel guilty, so they will give more of their hard-earned money, so they, the preachers, can increase their lifestyles. Remember, we are not under the law any longer; we are under Grace. Grace exposes the heart. If our hearts are right, we will give with a cheerful heart, we will give according to how the Lord has blessed us, be it five percent, ten percent or even twenty percent and beyond.

But you make that decision, not the preacher. Of course, we should give to our local church. But you get to decide how much you will give, when you will give, and to whom you will give. This is what the preachers said, sisters and brothers, and I believe them. You make your own choice. Grace. Learn grace and start giving.'"

"Amen," said Forrest.

The meeting continued with many members literally racing to the microphones asking questions about the letter: Was what the letter said true? Did God really want them to stop tithing? Who had written the letter? To this question, there was no answer. Nobody seemed to know who had penned the letter, but many were grateful.

The questions from the members, and the answers from Assistant Pastor Forrest, continued for another two hours or so.

The members of First St. Marks went home with many unanswered questions on their minds.

Most of them had a sleepless night.

Gaston Davis and two of his special committee members did not go home after the meeting of the Saints of First St. Marks Missionary Baptist Church. They stopped at a restaurant, had a light lunch, and then headed for the mansion.

Chapter Fifty-Four

"What was that all about, Son? What did you think you were doing?" Ben asked.

He and Forrest were on their way home. Forrest was driving.

Ben glared at his son in disbelief. "You've ruined everything!"

"No, I haven't, Dad. We are cleaning up some of the corruption that has been going on at First St. Marks. That's what we're doing, and it's about time."

"That letter. Did you write it? Did you send that to the members?"

"No, I didn't, Dad, but I'm glad someone did."

"Then who sent it?"

"I really don't know," Forrest said.

"Did we get a letter?" Ben asked.

Forrest hesitated for a moment. Yes, they had gotten a letter, but he had not shown it to his father, because he did not want him to get in the way of what had to be done. "Yes," he said.

"Then why didn't you show it to me?"

"I didn't show it to you, because I didn't want you to confer with Davis about it. I wanted the congregation to digest its contents, and then make their own decisions about their money."

"That was not your decision to make. I am the pastor, and I should have known about that letter!"

"I know, and I'm sorry I deceived you like that, Dad, but this was crucial. Would you have allowed the letter to be read?"

"No, because now they won't pay their tithes. We wanted them to pay the twenty percent."

"Why, Dad, because Davis commanded it, right? You, the pastor, did not want your congregation to hear the contents of that letter, because Davis wants more money to put into his pockets, right?"

"You don't understand!" Ben shouted.

"I understand that the church is being hustled by Davis and his underhanded committee, and that the pastor has become one of them. That's what I understand. Someone has to fight for the people of First St. Marks, Dad."

"But we can't do that."

"Why, Dad? Why not? As you said, you are the pastor. Don't you think that should be your responsibility?"

"I can't."

"You can't! You can't!" Forrest shouted. They had arrived at the mansion. Forrest hit the garage door button, the door went up, and he drove the Mercedes into the driveway and on into the garage. He hopped out of the car, hurried to the door leading from the garage into the house, unlocked it, hit the button to close the garage door, and went on into the house, leaving the door ajar for his father.

Ben hurried after his son. "I, I don't know what to do, Son. I, I . . ."

"You had an opportunity to redeem yourself in the eyes of your parishioners. What happened to you at the church this morning, Dad? Why didn't you answer Sister Rockford's question?"

"I was confused. If you had shown me the letter . . ."

"And watch you run straight to Davis with it? I don't think so," Forrest said as he led the way into the kitchen.

Ben sat in a chair at the table.

Forrest opened the cabinet door under the sink and pulled out a gallon can of lighter fluid. He then got a box of matches from a drawer beside the stove. "I'm grilling steaks for lunch." He washed his hands at the sink and then went to the refrigerator and took out a package wrapped in brown butcher paper and a bottle of marinade.

"Did Davis get a letter?" Ben asked.

"No, he didn't and neither did his special committee members, but apparently someone had told Davis about the letter by the time he got to the meeting this morning," Forrest said as he walked over to the sink and unwrapped the package that held two good-sized steaks.

"That's not right. He's the chairman of the Deacon Board. He should have gotten a letter."

"Apparently someone knew what they were doing," Forrest said as he washed the steaks.

"But the twenty percent . . ."

"They shouldn't be tithing, Dad. Be it ten or twenty percent, Christians should not be tithing. That's what Sister Rockford and I were explaining to the church body at the meeting."

"But they have to do it, Son, or we won't get the house! I want my house!"

Forrest dried the steaks with paper towels, put them in a glass dish, and then began pouring marinade over them. "Dad, this is more important than you having this house. This is about us robbing our members: a practice that must be stopped. This is about our integrity; this is about running First St. Marks like a church should be run." He sighed, his frustration rising. "Do you remember Reverend Ronald Joiner, the minister from Eagle Rock Baptist?"

"Yes, I remember him. He didn't practice tithing at his church, but that was his choice."

"That's right, and he told us some of the very things that were in that letter. I just didn't pay attention, and I guess you didn't either," Forrest said as he put the dish with the steaks into the refrigerator.

"But Davis said—"

"I don't care what Davis said! If we are going to pastor First St. Marks, we need to do right by our parishioners! After I got that letter, I began studying the Bible. I mean really studying it, the various chapters on tithing . . . I called Reverend Joiner, and read the letter to him. Dad, he is in total agreement with what we heard this morning. He said we are not under the old laws anymore, that we are under grace—just like the letter said. I should have known that, Dad, and so should you. Or did you know, and you chose to not govern your ministry accordingly, because you wanted to put as much money as possible in your pocket, just like the rest of all those other greedy ministers all over the country? Is that it, Dad?"

"No, I, I . . ."

The doorbell rang.

"Who could that be?" Forrest asked.

"I don't know. Suppose its Deacon Davis. He was so angry at the church. He might . . ." Ben left the sentence dangling.

"If it is Davis, we will deal with it," Forrest said as he went into the living room to answer the door. He opened it, and sure enough there stood Davis, Miles, and Clark. Davis carried his briefcase.

"My key didn't work in the door," Davis said, holding up a key for Forrest to see, his voice angry.

"That's because I changed the locks," Forrest said.

"How dare you, you impertinent—" Davis began as he stepped up into the room with the other men following.

"This is where I live, and I need to feel safe in my own home," Forrest said, interrupting him.

"This is the church's house," Davis corrected him.

"As long as my father and I are staying here, this is our home, and we need to protect ourselves in our home, especially in the middle of the night when other people might think they have a right to enter our home and roam about as they please—like the night Ms. Cooper ended up in my bed trying to rape me. Did you know about that, Davis? Did you just happen to lend her your key for that little adventure?"

Davis, Miles and Clark looked at Forrest disbelievingly.

"How dare you!" Davis shouted.

"Answer the question, please," Forrest said.

"Of course, I didn't . . . Oh, my God!" Davis exclaimed.

"Oh, you didn't know about that? You didn't know that the hooker you hired to seduce my father wants to play around with my father and me?" said Forrest.

"I don't know what you're talking about," Davis said.

"Oh, yes, you know, Davis, and I know all about what you are doing: the money, the scheming, the—" Forrest began.

"Who is it, Son?" Ben said as he walked into the living room, interrupting Forrest. "Oh, Deacon Davis, Deacon Miles, Brother Clark."

"And you . . ." Davis said as he whirled about to face Ben. "Why didn't you tell that woman she was out of order reading that letter this morning? Why didn't you take charge like the pastor you are supposed to be?" He slapped Ben.

Ben grabbed the side of his face where Davis had hit him; Forrest grabbed Davis by the arm, twisted it behind him, and shoved the man into the wall beside the door. "If you ever touch my father again, I'll finish what Brother Rockford started at the church this morning!"

"Get him off me," Davis yelled.

Miles and Clark pulled Forrest off Davis. Davis spun around and hit Forrest in the face. Blood spurted from Forrest's nose.

"Stop, stop!" Ben yelled.

"On the floor! Put him on the floor—face first!" Davis yelled.

Miles and Clark grabbed Forrest.

Forrest began quoting the Bible. "'*As for me, I will call upon God; and the Lord shall save me,*'"

The men wrestled Forrest to the floor.

"Stop, you're hurting him!" Ben yelled.

Forrest continued quoting the Bible. "'*Wickedness is in the midst thereof . . . Destroy Oh, Lord, and divide their tongues . . ..*'"

Davis straddled Forrest and hit him on the side of his face.

"Stop, stop!" Ben continued yelling.

"You wrote the letter, didn't you?"

"No, I didn't," Forrest said. "But I'm glad somebody did! *'Let death seize upon them, and let them go down quick into hell . . .'*" He continued.

Davis hit him again.

"Make him stop! Make him stop!" Ben said to the other men who just stood watching now.

"Come hold him down while I tape his wrists." Davis ordered the other men.

"I'm out of here, Davis! You've gone too far," yelled Miles.

"I'm leaving, too, Davis. Come on; we need to go," said Clark.

"No! You're both in this as deeply as I am. You're accomplices. What do you have to lose now?"

"My soul," said Miles. He opened the front door, and he and Clark started out of the house.

"We're leaving, Davis. Come on. Let's get out of here!" Clark shouted.

"No, you come back here! Do you hear me?"

Clark closed the door behind him and Miles.

"Then go! I don't need you!" Davis yelled as he continued struggling with Forrest.

"'*He shall send from heaven, and save me from the reproach of him that would swallow me up,*'" Forrest continued quoting the Bible.

Davis turned to Ben. "Come help me hold him down."

"No, no!" Ben said. "Let him go. Let him go!"

"I can't. You want the mansion, don't you?"

"Yes, I want the mansion," Ben said.

"And you want to marry Conswella, don't you?"

"Yes, yes, I want to marry her."

"Then come help me!"

"But . . ."

"Don't do it, Dad! Don't!" Forrest yelled to his father. "'*Deliver me from mine enemies, O my God; defend me from them that rise up against me.*'"

"He doesn't want you to marry her, remember? Help me tape his hands, and then I'm going to get your bride," Davis said.

"No, Dad! No! Don't listen to him," Forrest yelled. "'*Deliver me from the workers of iniquity, and save me from bloody men.*'"

Ben knelt down beside Davis and held his son's hands together. Davis opened his briefcase and took out a roll of duct tape.

"No!" shouted Forrest. "No, Dad. No! '*Deliver me from mine enemies, O God; defend me from them that rise up against me.*'"

Davis taped Forrest's hands behind his back and then he and Ben stood. Forrest looked up at his father in disbelief. "Dad . . ."

Davis chuckled. "Come on. Help me get him into the other room. Then I want you to go put on your tuxedo. I'm going to get your bride. We'll come back for you in a few minutes. I'm taking you to get married today, and I'm also going to bring you the deed to the house today," he said to Ben. Davis bent down and put his hands under Forrest's left armpit.

Ben put his hands under his son's other armpit, and he and Davis lifted Forrest to a standing position. They began to move forward. "Move," Davis shouted to Forrest, but Forrest refused to cooperate. He went completely limp. The two men had to struggle to get him into the parlor where they deposited him in front of the sofa. Davis then taped Forrest's hands to one of the legs of the sofa.

"Go get dressed," Davis ordered Ben. "I'm taking the Mercedes."

"I'll get the key," Ben said.

"Don't bother. I have one," Davis said.

"We should call the police," Miles said to Clark as they drove back into town.

"Are you crazy?" Clark asked. "We'd be in prison before we'd know what was happening."

"We have to do something, Clark. Davis is crazy. There's no telling what he might do."

"They've got two against one now. They'll be all right," Clark said.

"Davis has a gun. If he kills that boy, it will haunt me for the rest of my life. I'm calling the police," said Miles.

"Take me home first, and give me an hour. I'm leaving town," said Clark.

"I can't. I have a wife and a family," Miles said.

"Good luck," said Clark.

Dr. Mildred Dumàs

Chapter Fifty-Five

Forrest sat, his head lifted toward the heavens. "Help me, Lord. Help me!" *God hath heard me; he hath attended to the voice of my prayer. Blessed be God which hath not turned away my prayer, nor His mercy from me.'"

It was approximately forty-five minutes since he had been left in front of the sofa in the parlor. He had scooted across the floor pulling the sofa behind him until he finally realized his efforts were of no use, because he could not free his hands.

He had begun to pray—incessantly.

Ben suddenly appeared in the doorway. He was dressed in his black tuxedo. "I'm sorry, Son, but you wouldn't cooperate."

Forrest just looked at his father and shook his head. "So, you're all dolled up to go marry the hooker? I told you, Dad. She was hired to seduce you, to mess up your head, to play with your mind. Well, it seems she has done an excellent job. Yes, she has!"

The doorbell rang.

"Oh, they're here," Ben said. He looked at his son and smiled. "I'm going to get married, Son." He turned and started out of the room. "I'm going to get married," he repeated as he went into the living room to answer the door.

The bell rang again.

"I'm coming," Ben said. He opened the door. Mother McDonald stood there.

"Hello, Pastor. I'm here to see Pastor Forrest. I've been trying to call him, but he's not answering his phone," she said as she brushed past him.

"But, I, I . . ." Ben stammered. "You have to leave, Mother McDonald."

"Help! Help me!" Forrest yelled. "Help me! I'm in the parlor!"

"What in the world?" Mother McDonald said as she hurried through the house.

"No, no, you can't go in there!" Ben yelled as he closed the front door and hurried after her.

"Help me! Please help me! I'm in the parlor!" Forrest continued to yell.

Mother McDonald rushed into the parlor. "Oh, my God!"

"Get the scissors. Over there in the drawer," Forrest said, pointing to a table across the room.

"You're hurt," Mother McDonald said upon seeing the blood all over the front of his clothes and on the floor. "You need to go to the hospital."

"It's just a nose bleed. I'll be all right. Hurry!" Forrest said.

"I've been trying to call you," Mother McDonald said as she walked over to the table.

"My phone is in my briefcase in the kitchen," Forrest said.

"This is Davis' work I assume," she said.

"Yes, he and two of his friends came by," Forrest said.

"You have to leave, Mother McDonald," Ben said again upon entering the room.

Mother McDonald got the scissors from the drawer, brushed past Ben, as she went back over to Forrest to cut the tape from around his wrists.

His hands freed, Forrest got to his feet. "Thank you," he said to Mother McDonald. He looked upward. "Thank you, Lord." He smiled. "I knew you wouldn't leave me."

"You have to hurry. I had a dream. Take your father and leave here. Now! Take the back road through the quarters. It leads to the highway." Mother McDonald said.

"No, no, I have to get married," Ben said.

"You have to leave this place!" Mother McDonald said to Ben.

"No!" Ben said.

Forrest ran into the kitchen and got his Bible, his briefcase, and his keys from the counter beside the refrigerator where he had laid them earlier. He then ran back to the parlor, and took his father's arm. "We have to go, Dad."

"No, I won't go," Ben said, jerking his arm away from Forrest's grip.

Mother McDonald took hold of Ben's other arm. "Let's get him out of here."

Forrest took his father's arm again, and they led the protesting man through the house to the garage. Forrest opened the passenger-side door of the Cadillac and tried to push his father inside. Ben broke loose and tried to run back into the house. Forrest grabbed him.

"Open the back door," he said to Mother McDonald.

She did. Forrest pushed his father over to the back door, said a silent prayer, and then hit him upside the head with his fist. Ben went limp, his head and shoulders falling onto the back seat of the car. Forrest pushed him as far as he could into the car, and then went around to the other side, opened that door, and pulled Ben the rest of the way across the back seat. He shut the door. Mother McDonald pushed Ben's feet into the car on the other side of the car, and then shut that door.

Forrest went back around to the driver's side of the car, and hugged Mother McDonald. "Thank you, Mother McDonald."

"You're welcome. Goodbye, my friend. God speed."

Forrest got into the car and started the motor. He looked up at Mother McDonald who still stood beside the car. "Did you write the letter?"

She just smiled, waved at him, and backed away from the car.

"God bless you," he said. He drove the car out of the garage, on around back of the house, and then turned right.

Mother McDonald got into her car and drove off, heading back into town.

Chapter Fifty-Six

Davis drove the Mercedes into the driveway of the mansion approximately ten minutes later. He got out of the car, popped the trunk, lifted his briefcase out of it, closed the trunk, and then went around to the passenger side. He opened the door, and helped Conswella out of the car. He smiled "Let's go get your husband."

She returned his smile. "I can't wait." She was dressed in a white wedding gown with a white veil, white shoes, with a small silver evening purse swinging over her shoulder.

They walked up to the front door. Davis rang the bell.

There was no answer.

Davis rang the bell again.

There was still no answer.

Davis looked at Conswella with a concerned look on his face. "Come on," he said.

Davis led the way back to the car. He opened the driver's side door and punched the garage door opener on the visor. The garage door opened. He noticed that the Cadillac was gone. He hurried to the door that led into the house, Conswella right behind him. He fumbled with his keys for a moment, found the right one, and opened the door.

At least he didn't change the lock on this one, he thought.

He punched the button to close the garage door then led the way into the house. "Ben! Forrest!" he yelled.

There was no answer. *Where could they have gone?* He thought.

They walked into the kitchen. Davis laid his briefcase on a counter, opened it and took out his gun. "Wait here," he said as he ran through the house to the Parlor.

It was empty.

He hurried back to the kitchen. "They're gone," he said.

"Where?" She asked.

"I don't know, but the car is gone." He said as he laid his gun on the counter beside his briefcase.

"What were you going to do with that gun," she asked.

"Don't worry about it," he said.

"Well, what are we going to do now?" she asked.

"We have to find them. You have to marry Benjamin, so you can inherit the house upon his untimely death."

"How long will it take for him to die?" she asked.

"That's not your concern," he said.

"Suppose we don't find them? You promised me the house."

"Oh, we're going to find them; we don't have a choice."

"But suppose we don't find them?"

"Then I'll have my lawyer falsify more documents saying you are married, so you can get the house, and then you can quick deed it to me."

"You want me to give my house to you? That was not in the plan. This house is supposed to be my reward for marrying the old fool."

"Did you really think I was going to just let you have this house? He was going to disappear. How do you think that was going to happen?"

"As you said, that's not my concern."

"My plan is to sell the house. It's worth quite a bit of money. I would make it worth your while. I'd give you a fourth of whatever we can sell it for."

"A fourth? That wouldn't be worth the time I've wasted with that old man."

"Half then, I need the money."

Conswella got up in his face. "No! You greedy bastard, this is my house, not yours, and I make the rules concerning my house. Maybe I'll just give you a fourth—if I decide to sell!"

He slapped her, knocking her around, her head and shoulders landing on the counter top behind her. She looked up at a block that held an assortment of knives. She pulled the biggest one out of the block, swung around, and shoved it into Davis' chest. His eyes grew wide, and then he fell forward. Conswella slid down the counter. Davis' head just missed the place where she had been standing.

He groaned. "Help me. Help me."

"Sure, I'll help you," Conswella said as she walked over to the counter where Davis' gun laid. She picked up the weapon, and then walked back over to him. "Sure, I'll be glad to help you." "This house is mine!" she said as she aimed the gun at his back and pulled trigger. "Mine!" she shouted again, as she shot him again. "Mine!" she said again as she shot him again.

Conswella put the gun into her purse. "Now, what am I going to do with this piece of trash?" She asked herself.

She spotted the can of lighter fluid on the counter. Maybe the house would come in handy after all. A good cover. "Why not, because if I can't have it, nobody will," she said to herself. *Then I can get back to my life driving a spanking brand-new Mercedes,"* she thought.

She walked over to Davis, got down on her knees, reached into his back pants pocket and pulled out his wallet. She opened it and took out a handful of bills. "Mister Bigshot, always loaded, weren't you?" she said to Davis. She smiled, and then rolled him over onto his back. She reached into his right pants pocket and pulled out his keys. She put the money and the keys into her purse, got up, and walked over to the counter where the lighter fluid sat. She picked up the can, opened it and began pouring the contents on the floor around Davis' body. She picked up the box of matches, struck one, and then threw it onto the floor. Flames shot up all around Davis.

Conswella backed out of the kitchen still carrying the lighter fluid and the book of matches. She went into the dining room, walked over to the window, struck a match, and held it to the bottom of the curtains. In a moment, the curtains were in flames. She went on into the living room and set fire to the curtains in that room. She then set fire to the curtains in the parlor and the downstairs bedroom.

The doorbell rang.

Conswella stopped and looked at the door. Who was it? Maybe the pastors had come back. Maybe . . .

In a moment, the bell rang again. "Police!" a male voice shouted.

The police? she thought. Now what was she going to do? Maybe she could go out through the garage, get into the car and speed assay. No, they would have her before she even got to the car. Maybe she could sneak out the back way. No. They were probably all around the house. She was petrified. What was she going to do?

"Open the door, or we're going to break it down." the male voice again.

Conswella started backwards up the stairs, pouring fluid from the can onto the stairs as she climbed. When she reached the top of the stairs, she sat down the can, struck another match, and threw it on the stairs. They began to flame. She picked up the can and ran down the upstairs hallway, darting in and out of rooms, setting fire to the curtains and bedclothes in all of the bedrooms. She ran back into the hallway, and circled the wide-open space pouring liquid from the can as she ran. She walked over to the window seat that sat between the twin bay windows that she liked so much.

This was hers, all hers.

The battering ram made its first attack on the front door.

Chapter Fifty-Seven

Ben stirred on the back seat.

Not yet, Forrest thought. He didn't want his father to wake up just yet. They had only traveled a few miles. The road was bumpy and had rocks strewn about it in spots. *He can't regain consciousness now. There's no telling what he might do,* he thought.

Forrest wanted to at least be out of town, on the freeway where he could drive at a speed that might deter his father from trying to jump out of the car.

The road veered to the right, and Forrest took the turn as fast as he could, and then hit the brakes—hard. "Oh, no!" he shouted. There was a fallen tree across the road.

Forrest looked in the back seat. His father appeared to be sleeping now. He leapt out of the car, ran over to the tree, and tackled it from the top end, pulling at the branches, moving it a few inches at a time. It wasn't a big tree, but it was still heavy. He finally managed to wrestle the fallen tree over to the side of the road.

Forrest turned back to the car. "Oh, God!" he shouted. The back door on the passenger side of the car stood open.

Forrest took off running back down the road. He knew what had happened, but he slowed his run when he reached the car just long enough to check the back seat. Sure enough, his father was gone.

Forrest had to catch him before he reached the mansion.

Then he looked up and saw fire in the distance. "Oh, my God." He moaned.

Chapter Fifty-Eight

She heard the sirens in the distance, and then they were there: the fire trucks, ambulances, and people running all over the place.

Conswella stood at one of the bay windows looking down at all the commotion in the yard. She assumed the police had called the fire department upon seeing the fire at the front window. They had also come into the house after breaking down the front door but had apparently gone back out to wait for the fire department.

They were all here now, at her house.

They had seen her in the window, and the firemen were now yelling for her to open the window and jump. She had been walking from one window to the other for the past few minutes thinking about what she should do.

She had killed a man. Had they found him yet? Would they think he had died in the fire? No, no, there were a stab wound and three bullet holes in his body, and she had put them there.

"There he is," she said to herself as she watched several of the firemen roll a gurney out of the house with what appeared to be a covered body. They put the gurney into one of the waiting ambulances.

"Good riddance," Conswella said as the ambulance sped away from the house.

⚜

Forrest caught up with Benjamin just as they neared the house. They stood now among the gathering crowd looking at the flames that were consuming their residence. Some of the church members were already there. They gathered around their pastors doing what they could to comfort them.

Ben spotted Conswella in the upstairs window. "My wife! I have to save my wife." He took off running toward the house.

Forrest raced after him along with one of the firemen.

"Stop, you can't go in there!" yelled the fireman.

"Oh, there's my husband-to-be. Look at him run. He must be coming to save me." Conswella laughed, as she watched the new event that was happening down in the yard. *What an idiot,* she thought.

Forrest and the fireman grabbed Ben at the same time and pulled him back as the flames leapt toward them.

"That's my wife up there," Ben protested, as the men struggled with him.

One of the firemen appeared outside the window where Conswella was standing.

"Stand back," he shouted.

She moved back from the window. He raised a hatchet and hit the window pane. It began to shatter. He kept at his task until the window was about clean of glass. He reached for her. "Come on, lady; let me get you out of there."

Conswella reached into her purse, pulled out the gun, and shot him. He fell backward.

They caught him down below in the net that had been set up for Conswella to jump into earlier. The paramedics were on him at once.

"The left shoulder," said one of the paramedics after a brief examination. "Let's get him to the hospital."

In a few moments, another ambulance sped away from the house.

Conswella picked up the book of matches from the window seat, struck one and threw it to her right; then she struck another and threw it to her left. Fire immediately flared up about her.

Although the firemen had been watering the house for some time, it was still too consumed to enter.

Conswella continued to look down at the spectators standing below in the yard. Only now, she was smiling.

The crowd in front of the house was enormous now. They all watched as the woman in the wedding gown, in the upstairs window of the mansion, was consumed by fire and as the mansion began to crumble about her.

Chapter Fifty-Nine

Ben was inconsolable after seeing Conswella die in the fire. A few minutes after the house crumbled, the third ambulance left the house with him and one of the deacons from the church who had volunteered to go along with him so Forrest could stay with the house.

"I'm so sorry, Forrest. I didn't know," Sylvia said. She stood beside her ex-fiancé now, tears welling in her eyes.

"Because you didn't believe me. You didn't trust me," Forrest said.

"I'm sorry. I should have been there to help you with him. Maybe I could have talked to him. Maybe . . ."

"Excuse me," Forrest said. He walked off leaving Sylvia looking after him, her tears flowing freely now.

Forrest joined Mother McDonald and Deacon Stanton who had just joined the throng of people.

"I guess you didn't get too far," Mother McDonald said.

"No, we didn't," Forrest said.

"Deacon Smarts told us what happened with your father," Stanton said.

"I guess it was a good thing he brought you back. You're free now," Mother McDonald said.

"But what do I do now?" Forrest asked.

"Come stay with me for a few days. We'll talk," offered Mother McDonald.

"Excuse me," Deacon Stanton said. He hurried over to where he saw Octavia Davis standing among a group of other ladies. Octavia was crying. He assumed the other ladies were trying to console her. He had heard that Deacon Davis had been killed in the fire. He, as many of the others gathered there, wondered what had happened in that house?

Stanton took Octavia by the elbow. "Excuse me, ladies. I think Sister Davis should go see about her husband. I'll take care of her now."

"Oh, of course," said one of the ladies.

"You go, girl," Octavia's best friend, Sister Morgan, whispered in her ear.

Stanton reached into his pocket, pulled out a crisp, white handkerchief, and handed it to Octavia. He released her elbow, put an arm about her shoulder, and pulled her close to his side. Octavia dried her eyes one last time and leaned into him.

Some of the members of First St. Marks had heard a few things about Deacon Stanton and the First Lady of Clarksville. This group of ladies, as well as many other members, hoped the rumors were true, because they knew that the rumors about their esteemed mayor and his many exploits were true.

The ladies backed off, and Stanton took Octavia aside. "You should go see about him," he said.

"I know," she said.

"Do you want me to go with you?"

"No. I'll call you later."

"I'll walk you to your car."

"This way," she said.

In a few minutes the couple stood beside her car. He helped her into the driver's seat and closed the door.

She rolled down the window. "I love you," she said.

"I know," he said.

She rolled the window back up, started the car, and drove away from him.

Stanton looked toward the heavens. "Lord, you know I don't ever wish anybody any ill will, but today, I just want to say *thank you*."

Chapter Sixty

For months, the town of Clarksville talked about the latest scandal that had assailed the First St. Marks Missionary Baptist Church. When the citizens of Clarksville thought they had heard the worst from that church, the church proved them wrong—again. The scandals just kept getting bigger and bigger. The corrupt deacons and trustees stealing from the church with the mayor of the town—that was also the head deacon at the church—leading that pack of thieves and then dying in the burning mansion; then the woman in the wedding dress, standing in the upstairs window of the burning mansion, that they heard was a prostitute and also a member of the church; and then some of the deacons and the head trustee going to prison; and the police looking for another one who skipped town . . . . Then there was the one, a Deacon Miles, that got off with a fifteen thousand dollar fine and community service because he had turned *whistle-blower* on that group of thieves.

Lord, have mercy!

What a mess, what a disgrace to the town. First St. Marks was a disgrace. Many of the town's people thought that church should pad lock its doors, and stop masquerading as a house of God.

It was a wonder that the good Lord had not struck all of those people dead.

But First St. Marks refused to die along with the scandal. Eight months after the Lizzie Cochran mansion burned to the ground with two of its members inside—leaving only the servant's quarters and the hanging tree out back standing—the church was thriving again under the leadership of a new pastor, the Rite Reverend Forrest Thomas.

After their assistant pastor had exhibited so much love, devotion, and compassion, to the members of First St. Marks at what the members of the church had begun referring to as the *unveiling of the tithing myth meeting*, the members knew they could not find a better pastor no matter how long they searched.

The members made it clear though that they never wanted the Reverend Benjamin Thomas to set foot inside their church again. But they did not have to worry about that, because Benjamin was so ashamed, he left town two months after the incident, going to live with his brother, William, in Cleveland. He drove the Cadillac, promising his son that he would be careful. He had made it to Cleveland safely, and father and son talked often.

Forrest did not want the luxury sedan, but the new chairman of the Deacon Board, Deacon Richard Stanton, and the new chairman of the Trustee Board, Brother Fred Taylor, had insisted that he keep the car since it was already paid in full, and the members of each board had agreed.

Forrest had also moved into the parsonage, but not before one of Frist St. Marks members—who was a builder—and his crew had added a master bedroom, a family room, a screened-in sun porch, and had given it a new paint job.

"Just in case you decide to get married and have a few children," the builder told Forrest.

Sylvia Madden had moved out of her parents' house into her own apartment, which was located in the city of Clarksville, during those eight months.

Dr. Mildred Dumàs

On the morning that she got up and began packing, her mother asked her, "Where are you going, sweetheart?"

"To fight for my man," Sylvia replied. She soon became a member of First St. Marks Missionary Baptist Church, and was immediately assigned the new director of the children's church. Forest was, as always, pleased with her work with the children. They talked quite frequently and had gone to dinner together at Jimmie's Soul Food Restaurant a few times.

Forrest had even performed his first wedding ceremony. Six months and one day after Deacon Gaston Davis died, his widow married Deacon Richard Stanton. The church was packed with well-wishers. It was a spectacular event.

Troy Meadows was totally devastated by what had happened eight months earlier. He was going to have to find another mentor.

The Assistant Mayor, Robert Ingram, was now the Mayor of the city of Clarksville. He was doing a decent enough job, and, as far as the people of Clarksville knew, he was a decent enough man. But they had thought Gaston Davis was a decent man, too, so they would just have to wait and see.

First St. Marks was thriving as never before with the members giving liberally, some even more than they had been giving before the tithing meeting. They were giving because they wanted to give, because it felt good to give, because they knew now that their money would be used for the purpose it was given, because their new pastor would see to it.

THE END